Bouregy
March '04
20.00

W9-BFS-083

MARLBOROUGH PUBLIC LIBRARY
MARLBOROUGH MA

MR. PERFECT

MR. PERFECT

•

Shelagh McEachern

AVALON BOOKS
NEW YORK

McE

© Copyright 2004 by Shelagh McEachern
Library of Congress Catalog Card Number: 2003097356
ISBN 0-8034-9644-3
All rights reserved.
All the characters in this book are fictitious,
and any resemblance to actual persons,
living or dead, is purely coincidental.
Published by Thomas Bouregy & Co., Inc.
160 Madison Avenue, New York, NY 10016

PRINTED IN THE UNITED STATES OF AMERICA
ON ACID-FREE PAPER
BY HADDON CRAFTSMEN, BLOOMSBURG, PENNSYLVANIA

Chapter One

If she hadn't misplaced her glasses it never would have happened.

Verrick rummaged through the boxes in her new apartment trying to find her coffeepot. Her glasses were somewhere in the bathroom or bedroom; she'd find them later. Right now she was starving and needed a morning cup of coffee.

Her movements echoed in the spacious apartment, sounding hollow in the empty space, only unpacked boxes littering the polished hardwood floor. At last, she found what she was looking for.

Most of the coffee grounds she spooned out landed in the percolator, the rest sprinkled down over the sides onto the stovetop burner.

The dangling tie of her favorite dressing gown stayed caught in the drawer where she'd found the spoon as she turned to grope about for the toaster.

"Damn." She yanked it free but didn't bother to retie it, her dressing gown left open, revealing her old-fashioned flannel nightgown beneath.

Shortsighted as she was, Verrick found a breadboard and knife and sliced a piece of bread, then crammed it into the toaster.

1

The smell of coffee perking wafted past her nose as she padded across the dining room in her well-worn slippers. She opened the drapes to see for herself "the magnificent view of morning sun on the water," the sales agent had raved about.

However, her blurred vision saw little more than a vast expanse of gray fog.

"Fine lot of good that does." She shrugged in frustration. The room was brighter now, but the sea view was yet to be appreciated. "Where did I leave those glasses?"

While she shuffled toward her bedroom in search of them, a pungent burning aroma drifted from the kitchen.

"Not again!" She gave one long resigned sniff and wrinkled her nose at the acrid smell. "Burning coffee grounds! I *must* put on my glasses first thing each morning."

As she hunted for her glasses, the crookedly-sliced bread got stuck in the toaster instead of popping up. Smoke billowed up from the burning toast, forming a blue haze just beneath the kitchen ceiling. All the while, the gurgling sounds of the bubbling coffeepot resounded through the beautifully-designed modern kitchen.

Her search was interrupted by a nightmarish-loud sound splitting the morning silence like an incessant air raid siren.

"Good Lord. What's that?"

The shrill noise set her nerve ends jangling, blaring into the cluttered space with no sign of stopping.

An insistent thunderous banging on her door added to the uproar.

Angrily she stomped to the door, not an easy task wearing an open flapping dressing gown, sloppy slippers and down a hallway strewn with crates and boxes.

She yanked the solid door open and glared into the perfectly-knotted tie of the man standing there. She was tall, but he was much taller. Thankfully, she was without her glasses, for if she'd had them on she would have seen the disdain in his glowering brown eyes and the censure in his arrogant smirk.

He wasn't flustered or disorganized or shell-shocked by the din. His voice was as crisp as the finely-tailored suit he was wearing.

"I believe you're having some problem with your smoke alarm." He formed every word slowly and carefully as if speaking to an idiot.

"Is that the horrible noise?"

The words were spoken to his immaculately well-dressed back as he swept past her into the kitchen, reached his long arm up to the ceiling and silenced the screaming horror.

Verrick sighed, rubbing her forehead, the beginning of a headache starting to throb through her hungry, unwashed, agitated self. She focused her eyes somewhere in the vicinity of the fashion-plate stranger who was unplugging her toaster. He turned on the fan above the stove and the smoky haze began to clear, although the sharp charred odor of burned coffee grounds still lingered.

Another more pleasant fragrance permeated her senses, a fresh male cologne. She remembered her manners.

"Thank you. I'm grateful the howling's been silenced."

His cold stare went over her head to survey the disarray of unpacked boxes and carelessly placed furniture. Then he fleetingly glanced at the disheveled woman, tumbled sandy hair, big blue eyes that seemed dazed and a shabby dressing gown and slippers most women would have thrown in the garbage.

Unsettled by his silence, Verrick stammered to explain. "I've just moved . . . in"

She couldn't clearly see his face but she did catch his haughty tone of voice. "Obviously."

He only said that one word but it slapped like a glove in her face. It was an insult. She didn't know what offended him most, the shambles of her apartment or the untidiness of her person.

"Have the manager reset that alarm."

It was an order, no friendly introductions, or neighborly chatter. She guessed he must be a neighbor—he got here quickly enough. She was dying for a cup of coffee and would have offered one to this tall streak of dark blue suit but he continued before she had a chance to open her mouth.

"Perhaps he can help you avoid another disaster like this morning." She could feel his scathing look as he muttered in a low voice, "But from the look of you, I doubt it."

With that, he pulled open the door and stepped briskly into the hallway, closing it carefully behind him.

Verrick leaned her back against the door, sweeping her hand across her forehead to smooth the uncombed hair out of her eyes.

"Good morning to you, too," she said sarcastically to the man who had so abruptly left without a word of welcome or a wish to make her acquaintance.

What a beginning. She shuffled to the coffeepot to finally pour herself a cup and start her day.

If she hadn't misplaced her glasses it never would have happened.

By nine o'clock, Verrick had eaten breakfast, showered and dressed—with her glasses firmly atop her nose. She had to agree with the sales agent, the morning sun on Semiahmoo Bay was magnificent. The long wooden pier stretched into the bay, stopping at the rocky breakwater sheltering the few boats docked in the mooring spaces at the end of the pier. Looking to the south, along the endless stretch of sandy beach, she could see the large white rock after which the town was named, and further south, the tip of Mount Baker, snow-covered and shrouded in clouds catching the first golden glints of morning sunlight.

Her view was unimpeded. She hardly needed to hang her fine collection of landscape paintings on the walls. The view beyond the wall of glass dazzled the eyes and filled her new home with cheery warmth and light.

A melodic doorbell chimed. Verrick smiled. Nice touch— no jarring buzzer from the downstairs entrance at Westerly

Place, instead, an elegant doorbell. She liked that. This place was designed with a touch of class.

"Yes . . ."

"Carter's Moving, ma'am. We have the rest of the load for Miss Grant."

Verrick released the main door lock. "Come up. It's 401 on the top floor."

She sent the moving crew home last night after they laid the carpet and placed the antique pieces of her bedroom suite to her satisfaction. The drapes were hung and all her clothing put on hangers in the huge closet. It was all so new and still smelled of cedar lining the inner wall. Only the bedroom was complete. The men were back this morning to finish the rest of the rooms.

She opened the door before the second knock.

"Morning, ma'am."

Finally, a pleasant greeting. The two men were young with ready smiles, wearing work clothes and heavy boots.

First, the Persian carpets went down, one in the living room and another in the guest bedroom. Then the big pieces were placed, the sofa and chairs, the dining room table and sideboard, and finally, the small tables, bookcases, lamps and boxes of kitchen utensils.

In spite of the impression she may have given her neighbor, Verrick was organized and creative. In a short time, the never-lived-in apartment looked warm and cozy, as though someone had made it home for years.

Verrick stood back, very pleased with the final result. She hadn't been too sure about that orangey shade she had the painters put in the living room. It was the delicious color of an orange ice cream cone but she feared it might be overpowering. Her fears were unwarranted; the color was exactly right, shifting from cream to peach to a delicate shade of sunset orange as the light changed throughout the day.

She took the moving crew out for lunch at a nearby restaurant, putting them at ease, comfortable and unpretentious, eating fish and chips with as much enjoyment as the two young men.

By three o'clock, everything was in its place. The two men had patiently held up paintings while Verrick stood back and positioned them just right. The brand new walls were smooth so the picture nails had to be in the right spot—she didn't want to scar the unmarked finish.

Pictures were hung, clothes neatly arranged in dresser drawers, dishes in the cupboards and chairs pushed in around the dining room table. Verrick watched the moving truck pull away from the loading zone in front of the new building. Already it felt like home, she knew it the instant she first stepped into the apartment. The architect of Westerly Place knew exactly what a real home needed and designed the building perfectly with everything she wanted.

The only puzzling space was that long, glassed-in room with the sky lights and hardwood floor. At the moment it was bare, narrow, almost like a bowling alley. She supposed it was meant to be a sun room or a sitting room or a place for growing lush indoor tropical plants. The only problem was—she had never kept a plant alive for more than a week. She had even killed plants that others considered weeds, watering too much or not enough, giving them too much sun or too much shade. Hers was the touch of death to house plants.

She loved plants and truly desired to have them thrive in her care. She looked at the polished floor of the empty, sun-washed room. This was the perfect spot for a garden room. Maybe now was a good time to get serious about developing a green thumb. Perhaps she should take a course in horticulture at the nearby college.

The door chime interrupted her visions of splendid flowering plants, lush and green with verdant health and spectacular blossoms.

"Yes."

"Verrick? This is the place? Wowee! It's posh."

"Come up, Jenna. Wait till you see the rest of it."

Almost as soon as Jenna pressed the elevator button, the doors slid noiselessly open. It was not empty. A man coming up from the underground parking garage watched her press the fourth floor. The doors swished closed and the elevator smoothly ascended to the penthouse floor.

Two more different people couldn't have occupied the small space. One was over six feet tall, conservatively dressed in a dark blue business suit. The other, almost a foot shorter, outrageously dressed, was as colorful as a gypsy, with a very short skirt, pierced nose and short spiky dark hair, streaked with purple.

She watched him look her over in the mirrored elevator. His straight face didn't twitch a muscle, no smile, no frown, no raised eyebrows. This actor was good, he could play the most wholesome innocent in the goriest horror film. He realized she knew he was studying her. She lifted her chin and looked directly into the mirror, meeting his candid dark eyes. She winked boldly, and as the elevator doors swept open, she swore she saw those ever so proper brown eyes wink right back.

He knew she had to be going to 401; there were only two penthouse apartments on this floor. He smiled as he unlocked his door; it had been years since he'd seen a pierced nose close up—not since his sister, Rachel, shocked the family with hers. They got used to it eventually, as Rachel pointed out, "There are far more daring body parts I could've pierced." He stepped into his silent apartment, catching the faint sound of happy female voices greeting each other at the far end of the hall.

"Verrick, this is splendid. And the light . . . incredible!"

"Come see the ocean view. It changes hourly, sun, shadow, clouds, wind—even the water color changes from muddy brown to murky gray, then sparkling silver atop greeny blue. I could sit all day and watch the shifting patterns and changing moods on the water."

"Boring! Girl, you've got to get out more."

The two friends laughed. They were closer than most sisters and had mercilessly teased each other from the day they met at boarding school.

"Who was the stuffed shirt in a business suit I came up in the elevator with?"

"I don't know. I haven't met any of my neighbors yet."

"You'll know when you meet this one—the tall, blonde, handsome type. I have a sneaking suspicion he's not as straight-laced as he appears."

"Just your type, then."

"Far from it—no tattoos, no body piercing, natural hair, no dye job. Too uninteresting for me."

"Don't be fooled. Under that suit might lurk the masterpieces of some funky tattoo artist or piercings in places you couldn't imagine."

"That's what I like about you, girl. You always believe the nicest things about people."

"Come see the mystery room. What do you make of it?"

"How romantic . . . a starlight ballroom."

"A ballroom?"

"Look . . . a wall of windows and the skylights. Imagine it under a full moon, clear sky, stars twinkling . . . and music to dance by. It's a ballroom, Verrick, no two ways about it."

"I was thinking more along the lines of a sunroom . . . you know . . . wicker furniture and lots of plants."

"Dull, dull, dull. You're getting old, girl."

"I'm two months older than you, old lady—thirty next birthday, so show some respect."

"If you're not in a hurry to do anything with your ballroom, could you leave it just as it is for several weeks?"

"It's bald—shiny wood floor, wall of glass, and no furniture."

"I want to give it its fifteen minutes in the spotlight."

Verrick Grant watched the cunning look on her friend's face as her eyes darted about the narrow room, scoping it out, taking mental notes and visual measurements.

"I'm searching out locations for a science fiction movie that plans to start shooting in two weeks. There's one scene where they visit the home of this brilliant scientist. No one has suspected, but he's a bit kinky. His personality hasn't been revealed to the audience yet, so his home is the first glimpse into his dark side."

"What do you have in mind?"

"Stark room, whips and chains, black leather, some far-out exercise equipment . . . that sort of thing. This would be perfect."

"I don't know . . ."

"Let loose, Verrick. Live dangerously. It's only a brief scene, could probably be shot in a single day. It won't disturb your toney neighbors, I promise."

"Okay. I agree, just remove all the weird stuff when you're finished."

"It's a deal."

"Now come into my kitchen and be dazzled. The designer put everything in the right place. I even have a dishwasher."

Over a dinner of grilled chicken and stir-fried vegetables, Verrick relaxed into her new home with Jenna, her first guest. The day had a shaky start but was ending on a friendly note. If walls had arms, these walls would be hugging her, it felt that welcoming.

Of course, she'd have to be careful not to misplace her glasses again.

After Jenna left, Verrick walked through the rooms, so different from this morning. She stopped in the middle of the empty room; there was no full moon, no twinkling stars, but Jenna had named it the Starlight Ballroom and the name fit. She chuckled as she walked through to her bedroom. "Just what I've always needed—my own private ballroom."

The next morning she woke early, well-rested and very pleased with her residence. She carried her coffee through to the sun deck facing the beach and watched the early morning joggers along the promenade sprinting past an elderly couple walking their dog.

She didn't have to be in the office until tomorrow morning, so she had one more day to settle in, shop for groceries and to speak to the building manager about resetting that alarm.

Wearing a cherry red sweater over white corduroy slacks, she felt energetic enough to skip down the four flights of stairs to the parking garage. Her allotted parking space was right beside the door and well-lit, the spot considered safest for a single woman. But she had to maneuver around a cement pillar to get in and out. She got into her dusty, dented car and backed up slowly. She wasn't sure if she'd completely cleared the pillar, so she pulled back into her parking space then backed up again, further this time so she wasn't in danger of ramming the cement post. Her old car tended to burn oil, so a cloud of smoke marked her progress, along with the rattles and coughs of a jerky start.

Not having turned her steering wheel quite far enough to aim directly at the exit gates, she pulled in once more and executed the turn perfectly this time.

Intent on avoiding the cement pillar, she hadn't noticed the tall blonde man unlocking his shiny Porsche in the parking space beside hers. Seeing his movements in her rearview mirror, she rolled down her window, smiled and said, "Good morning."

The response wasn't exactly a smile, more a grimace.

"As adept with a car as you are with a toaster, I see."

That didn't deserve a reply. She gritted her teeth, stepped on the gas and zoomed out the gates.

Her neighbor didn't merit polite conversation. That was the last good morning he'd hear from her.

But Verrick didn't see the laughter sparkling in the depths of those dark-lashed brown eyes. "Feisty thing. My new neighbor has a temper."

As he swung his silver Porsche onto Marine Drive, he listed the attributes of the unknown woman—great hair, framing her face in natural waves with a tendency to curl, lovely cornflower blue eyes, not quite masked by her glasses, flawless complexion and full lips—a step above the newly wed and half-dead his brother predicted would be his only neighbors if he moved to White Rock.

She didn't seem to be newly wed; and she was far from half-dead.

He merged onto the freeway and headed into Vancouver. *I wonder what her name is.*

As Verrick emptied grocery bags to stock her refrigerator and pantry shelves, she happened to look up at the offending fire alarm that shrilly split her morning calm the previous day. She remembered she must speak to the building manager about resetting it.

And that brought to mind the neighbor of hers—obnoxious man, too perfect to be believed. "Mr. Perfect" she named him in her mind. This morning she got a good look at him with her glasses on—her first impressions hadn't been wrong. The guy was tall, a physical specimen with blonde hair and a mustache. Surprisingly, his eyebrows were dark and his eyes were brown.

Of course, *he* could pull out of his parking spot without hesitation on the first try and come nowhere near scraping the cement pillar.

And he knew how to silence the alarm, too. It wasn't fair he looked that good so early in the morning, his clothes were impeccable, flawlessly pressed, even his shoes shone. And that hair, slightly long, touching his collar but every strand in place, nothing mussed about him.

For emphasis, she struck the fist of her right hand into the palm of her left with a loud thwack. *I'd love to muss that man's teeth.*

"Good day, Miss Grant. Are you all moved in?"

"Yes, thank you, Mr. Stephenson. I need help with the smoke alarm. Would you be able to reset it for me?"

"Of course. But first, have you had a chance to tour the whole of Westerly Place?"

"Briefly, with the sales agent." The middle-aged man looked eager to familiarize her with the luxurious structure under his care. She flashed him a smile. "I'd love to have a closer look."

Mr. Stephenson proudly pointed out the architectural details, the native plants used in landscaping, the courtyard with appropriate benches and a remarkable climbing gym and slide for children. Verrick had a soft spot for playground equipment, she couldn't resist climbing the ladder and zipping down the slide to land in the soft sand at its base.

"Are there any children living in the building?"

"No, I'm afraid not. Many of the residents have grandchildren who enjoy a safe place to play outdoors. You can't be too careful these days, can you?"

Verrick nodded, pleased but curious why an upscale development like this made accommodations for children when none lived here.

The building manager could read the questions on her expressive face. "The architect has a liking for children. He includes an original play space in all his projects, even office towers."

"Nice touch."

Mr. Stephenson beamed, then leaned forward to confide in hushed tones, "You're the first adult to try the playground equipment. The rest of us only admire it."

Verrick laughed. "Live dangerously, Mr. Stephenson. Sneak out at midnight and give it a try."

"I'd never do that, Miss."

"I won't tell," she whispered. "I can personally recommend it."

The manager laughed at the youngest resident of the exclusive building. For a professional woman, she had a joyful sense of fun. She would fit in nicely.

Verrick admired the design refinements he pointed out, it really was a marvel.

"Did you know this development has been nominated for an architectural award?"

"I'm not surprised."

"Both the builder and the architect are to be honored. Not many condominiums can boast a guarantee against leaks."

"Can this one?"

Mr. Stephenson gave her a scolding glance. "Most definitely, Miss Grant. No structure put up by either the builder or the architect has ever leaked. They stake their reputations on it."

"I didn't realize that. But I could have guessed, there's obvious attention to detail in every aspect."

That was the right thing to say. Mr. Stephenson fairly glowed with pride as he led the way to the elevator.

"Would you object to having the judging committee look through your apartment, Miss Grant? They will be coming to make an assessment sometime soon. I'm sorry I can't be more specific."

"Feel free to show them through . . ." she was going to add "in my absence" but the elevator door slid silently open and the glaring eyes of her meticulous neighbor raked over her.

The building manager spoke first. "Mr. Parford, have you met the newest resident of Westerly Place?"

A chilling scowl descended from his superior height onto Verrick's cheery red sweater and sandy white corduroys. A deep voice tinkling with shards of ice answered Mr. Stephenson. "We've met, but we haven't been introduced."

Oh, Verrick grimaced inwardly. *The pompous ass! Does he expect me to bow and produce my business card?* He must be ancient—only people old enough to be grandparents were that stiff and formal.

Mr. Stephenson had none of her reservations, he was

delighted to see the man. In fact, he treated him like some superior being.

"Then allow me to introduce you. Mr. Parford, this is Miss Grant."

He would have said more, but Mr. Perfect extended his hand and said, "Pleased to meet you."

Those words must have nearly choked him because he seemed to be swallowing hard and holding his face rigid, likely in fear it would shatter in case he broke into a smile.

Verrick politely shook his hand. She wasn't going to lie and say she was pleased to meet him.

"Charmed, I'm sure," she said insolently, mimicking the most arrogant of British high society.

The man's cheeks twitched but he didn't say a word. His eyelids lowered over those critical eyes and he stepped into the elevator.

Verrick and Mr. Stephenson continued along the hallway to adjust her smoke alarm.

Only when the elevator door closed, did Lionel Parford release the burst of laughter he was holding back. "Charmed, I'm sure!" *The woman's a comedian.*

As he crossed the pavement to his car, he chuckled. He hadn't missed the sand clinging to the bottom and cuffs of her white corduroys. The woman had probably been playing in the sand. He wouldn't put it past her.

"Charmed, I'm sure," he repeated again to himself and grinned all the way to the building site he was going to see.

Chapter Two

V errick managed to avoid contact with the man for the
rest of the week, quickly going to the elevator on her way
to work in the morning and just as quickly returning in the
evening, always fearful the elevator door would swoosh
open and she'd see the face of her blonde neighbor staring
down at her. She didn't stop to question why his presence
bothered her so . . . she just knew it did. Thankfully, she
didn't catch a glimpse of the perfectly groomed man.

That's not to say he didn't see her. He watched her softly
pad down the hallway, a seductive sway to her hips and a
graceful poise to her movements.

Her clothes were distinctive. She wore soft, soothing pas-
tels and florals, all very feminine, none of the strident
black, blood red, and bilious green he encountered in down-
town offices. Her clothing was gentle and calm. Perhaps
she worked with women. Maybe she was a hairdresser or
something like that. She didn't wear a uniform, some days
he'd seen her in slacks, but this morning she was wearing
a soft rose colored skirt that swirled around her knees. The
woman had legs. Boy, did she ever! Long shapely legs and
delicate ankles. And she wore sensible shoes, none of those
high-heeled horrors that near crippled a woman. She must
spend the day on her feet.

Miss Grant was definitely intriguing.

"Verrick, have you made plans for Thanksgiving yet?"

"No, Jenna. You know my mother doesn't cook so I won't be going there for turkey dinner. How about you?"

"My parents are in Winnipeg. My brother's wife had a new baby. I thought we could cook dinner at your place, use the starlight ballroom and make a housewarming out of it."

"We?"

"Ralph and myself and a few others."

"How many others?"

"All our friends without families close by . . . maybe ten . . . twelve."

"Are you planning to help with the cooking?"

"I'll make pumpkin pies and Ralph can whip cream."

"Okay. I'll order a fresh turkey."

"Speaking of turkeys . . . have you met your stuffed shirt neighbor, yet?"

"We met alright." Verrick gave an exact imitation of Lionel Parford's lofty tone saying, "We have been introduced."

Jenna giggled. "How old is this guy?"

"I don't know. I didn't see his teeth."

"Spoken like the dentist you are. Verrick, you judge a horse's age by its teeth. This isn't horse flesh you're looking at."

"You can tell a lot about a person by their teeth."

"You spend too much time looking into people's mouths. You're not buying a horse."

"I wouldn't want him even if he had four legs. The man makes me jittery. He's pretty tight-lipped, he hasn't flashed his pearlies at me."

"Jittery? You? Where's the confident doctor who drills into people's teeth and never flinches?"

"That's easy, Jenna. I know what I'm doing in the dentist office. I haven't a clue how to deal with my neighbor. It might be easier if he seemed friendly, at least more approachable."

"Hasn't he given you even one little smile?"

"Oh no, not one. He glowers at me."

"What does he do for a living?"

"I don't know."

"Should we invite him for Thanksgiving?"

"Heaven forbid! He'd never accept an invitation from me and besides, I'd be a nervous wreck with him at the table."

"We can't have that. Why does this guy turn the confident Dr. Grant into a quaking ninny?"

"Jenna! He rattles me, that's all. I'll get over it."

"I hope so." Jenna smiled to herself, she suspected an attraction Verrick Grant was unwilling to acknowledge. She said no more about it.

"By the way, your starlight ballroom has the go ahead as a scene location for that movie I mentioned. Ralph can look it over for lighting and test for sound. It'll be great."

"Fine by me. I haven't started raising plants or buying wicker furniture yet."

"Does your neighbor have a starlight ballroom?"

"I suppose so. He has the other penthouse suite on this floor, I'd guess its floor plan is similar to mine."

"What has he done with his?"

"Beats me. Something perfect, no doubt."

The late September weekend weather remained warm, the breeze light. Sun sparkled off the water, inviting Verrick to come down to the beach and enjoy the glorious stretch of smooth sand.

Once across the train tracks and onto the sand, she took off her sandals and rolled up the legs of her jeans. The tide was way out, so with sandals dangling from one hand, she set out barefoot toward the water's edge, wading through warm shallow pools, watching sandpipers running across the sand searching for food, and seagulls fighting over scraps of fish. A fishing boat was heading out in the distance but few people were about on the beach this morning. At least it seemed that way. The sand stretched out as far as she could see, even with hundreds of people it would seem almost deserted.

Verrick stopped and watched a boy fling a stick for his dog to chase. The big dog splashed through sea water pools, captured the stick in his teeth, and raced back to his owner, shaking off sand and water, anxious to do it all over again.

She walked a long while to reach the ocean's edge, sloshed about in the cool salt waves for a bit, then turned back toward shore. The sun was getting higher in the sky now and more people were arriving at the beach. She could see some strolling along the pier and others spreading blankets and settling on the sand, children with plastic spades and buckets and adults with picnic baskets and the latest bestsellers.

The houses of White Rock stretched up the hill, some clinging to the cliff in several levels, all facing the sea with a panoramic ocean view. As she neared the paved promenade, she could see the serious morning joggers keeping pace, feet pounding rhythmically, elbows bent, backs straight. She admired their fluid movement as they blurred along the promenade, a smear of colorful shorts, bronzed legs and white running shoes.

The sun was getting warm. She hadn't worn sunglasses and was squinting into the light. Her T-shirt was damp and sweaty and streaked with sand where she'd brushed her hands across it. There was a fishy smell in the air, the sun beginning to bake the sand and tidal pools, releasing their distinct aroma.

A fierce-looking dog with the appearance of a wolf, gray with black markings, came racing along the path beside its owner. Verrick had never been comfortable with dogs, especially not ones with huge yellow teeth and lolling tongues like this one. With the sun in her eyes, she nervously jumped out of its path, smack into the solid chest of a jogger.

Her first impression was of a dry, crisp white shirt, smelling of sunshine and spring breezes so unlike her own. He put out his hands to steady her, holding her by the shoulders, preventing her from toppling over.

It was then she looked all the way up to the collar of the freshly laundered shirt. Who but Mr. Perfect?

She gulped, blinked, then stared.

"Not a dog lover, I see."

She looked down beside him. That wolf-like dog was licking the hand he extended and wagging its tail. If dogs could smile, this one was smiling. When he said, "Sit," the dog sat.

Verrick exhaled a sigh of relief.

"Is this dog yours?"

"No. He belongs to that jogger in the red shorts. He'll wait here until his owner returns."

"Then you've been introduced?"

He bit his cheeks to keep from grinning. "Indubitably."

This was ridiculous. They sounded like two Victorian spinsters.

"I apologize for bumping into you, Mr. Parford."

"Think nothing of it, Miss Grant."

She was on the verge of curtsying. If she'd had a fan, she'd have fluttered it in front of her face.

Instead, she said, "Good day." Then Verrick stepped past him and walked in the direction of home in as ladylike a fashion as possible, barefoot, carrying her sandals, her pant legs rolled up, and liberal smatterings of sand and salt water plastering her clothes to her skin.

She didn't look back to see him resume his jogging pace.

Her knees felt shaky just thinking about him. He was too good to be true, he didn't even sweat.

Verrick stood under the hot shower until every particle of sand had washed down the drain. She shampooed her hair and rinsed until it was squeaky clean. Then she filed her nails, a weekly ritual, she liked them neatly trimmed for work. It wouldn't do to scratch her patients.

Darren was taking her to a play this evening, a production by White Rock Players. She hadn't seen their work before, but she'd heard they were good.

Since she and Jenna were in grade school, they'd both loved the theater, painting scenery, placing microphones, adjusting lights, singing in the chorus, and later, taking on serious acting roles.

It was a way to escape, pretending to be someone else, living a make-believe life. Verrick took to it like a duck to water. Acting in plays, she'd been able to experience the home life she never had, the parents she wished she had, adventures she'd never consider in real life, and all the dreams any young girl could imagine. Pretending had saved her sanity.

Jenna had pursued a career in the performing arts, working for a film company, spotting locations and working her way into directing short films. Verrick was more conservative. Acting was fun, but not as a career. She didn't want to live in the spotlight. Being her mother's daughter caused more than enough notoriety for her. She dreamed of a quiet life, cozy home, white picket fence, children, grandparents and a real family, not the lonely vagabond existence she'd grown up with.

She dressed carefully and was ready when her doorbell rang. She loved that touch, an actual doorbell. It felt homey, like a house in the suburbs, the kind she'd never lived in.

The play was fun and Darren was his usual undemanding company. They'd met in university, shared common interests and remained firm friends ever since, never as intimate as Darren had hoped, but friends just the same.

"Do you regret moving out of Vancouver?"

"No. My practice is here in White Rock. I'm enjoying the small town and slower pace."

"Not for me. It's miles from anywhere."

"I like it. I should've made the move sooner."

"Just a country girl at heart, eh, Verrick?"

"Something like that."

He held her hand as they left the theater and walked the short block to the restaurant where he'd made reservations for dinner.

"Dr. Harris is organizing another flight into the coastal towns and isolated Indian villages. Are you included this time, Verrick?"

"Yes. I manage a four-day weekend once every few months. How about you?"

Darren shook his head. "I told Bob Harris to count me out. The conditions are primitive, it's hard to do good work. And I got airsick in that float plane. I haven't the stomach for missionary work, I'm afraid."

Verrick smiled. "Dr. Harris is dedicated, and the work is appreciated. Without him, a great many people would have no access to dentists or medical care."

Darren leaned across and kissed her cheek. "Soft-hearted Verrick. You can't save every suffering soul you meet, you know."

"I can try."

"But you'll burn yourself out, love." He stroked her hand where it lay on the tablecloth. Darren knew about her being an only child shipped off to boarding school as young as one would take her. She was a sucker for any child with sad eyes. "You can't save them all, love. You have to look after yourself, too."

"Yes, doctor." She grinned and gave an accurate impersonation of her mother. "Honey lamb, you've got to reach right out and grab what you want. No one's going to hand it to you."

Darren saw behind the humor. "How is Elly?"

"Last I heard, she's divorcing husband number five."

He held both her hands and met those soulful blue eyes straight on. "Still hurt?"

"Not really. Occasionally I have a bout of 'wouldn't it

have been nice if . . .' but usually I can accept my parents for what they are."

"Good girl. Have you overcome your aversion to marriage yet?"

"Not yet. Watching my parents go at it, I haven't much faith in marriage as a lasting institution."

"When you change your mind, remember I'm still here."

"You're a dear. But don't hold your breath waiting."

"Honey lamb, if I'd held my breath waiting for you to marry me, I'd have turned blue and died of asphyxiation years ago."

Verrick squeezed his hand. "I'm glad we've got that straight."

"You've never been anything but honest with me, love. I can't complain about that."

A spectacular sunset of rosy pinks and mauve washed across the sky, reflected back by the still water of Semiahmoo Bay. Gradually the colors darkened as the sun slipped below the horizon, and night took over. The lights on the pier flickered and the streetlights lit the roadway. Darkness had descended over the water, but still people moved along Marine Drive. The restaurants were doing a thriving business on an unusually warm, dry September night.

Gavin Parford looked down from his brother's solarium onto the dark street below. A sleek Mercedes pulled up in front of Westerly Place and stopped. A suave gentleman walked around the hood and opened the passenger door to help a woman onto the sidewalk.

"Who's the babe?"

Lionel Parford joined his brother and looked down onto the street. "My neighbor."

"What's her name?"

"Miss Grant."

Gavin was surprised by his brother's somber expression as his eyes studied the scene playing out on the street below. He couldn't resist provoking his unflappable older brother. "She's a beauty."

"She cleans up well."

Gavin laughed. "That's all you have to say? She cleans up well? Tell me, what's her whole name."

"I don't know."

"You don't know? The only person beside yourself living in this building under the age of ninety-five, and you haven't found out her first name! Lion, you can't be king of the beasts if you don't make a move."

He saw the driver of that late model Mercedes kiss Miss Grant as he left her at the entrance door, not a passionate kiss, but he kissed her. It wasn't like him to be brusque, but he turned on his younger brother and snapped, "I'm not about to leap on every woman that crosses my path."

Gavin waggled his eyebrows. "Finding out her name doesn't require leaping on her."

Lionel grumbled some reply and walked back into the sitting room.

His younger brother hadn't forgotten the exchange. When he left, he patted Lionel on the shoulder. "I'll tell you her name when I find out."

This parting comment was answered with the crisp snap of Lionel Parford's door being slammed shut.

Verrick discovered that the private swimming pool and sauna at Westerly Place were deserted each evening when she returned from work. So every day, rather than rushing to prepare dinner, she slipped into her bathing suit, tied on a beach robe, and grabbed a towel. The pool was delightful, light and airy, tucked into a corner of the building, not too big, nicely heated, and she had it all to herself. Luxury.

She swam leisurely laps for half an hour, relaxing into each stroke, gently stretching her arms, shoulders and back, supported by the warm water. Her colleagues complained of back pain, aching legs and sore muscles from bending over the dentist's chair. Swimming was the perfect exercise for tired muscles, Verrick figured a little prevention was worth the time spent to avoid discomfort later.

It was a peaceful escape and she glided through the water, unwinding and working up an appetite, planning the dinner she would cook after she towelled off.

The following Friday was no exception to her routine. Jenna was to join her for dinner and she'd told her friend to bring a bathing suit. But there was a difference.

When the two women shuffled into the pool room in their loose flapping beach thongs, someone else was swimming laps. Not slow leisurely laps, but vigorous, rapid laps—the kind you see in Olympic competitions.

"Who's that?" Jenna asked in a low voice.

"I can't see. My contact lenses aren't in and I don't have my glasses."

"Looks like some athlete in training, swims like a torpedo."

"A torpedo?"

"Yeah, fast and lethal."

The swimmer was alerted by the sound of the glass door sliding open and then he heard the murmur of women's voices. This had been his private haven these past weeks, no one else in the building seemed to be a swimmer, at least not in the evenings. He slowed his pace, lifted his head to look up at a long length of gorgeous leg, topped by a short beach jacket. He shook his head, clearing his eyes and splattering water from his slicked-back hair.

"Uh-oh," Jenna whispered. "It's that neighbor of yours."

Verrick would have turned and left but he swam to the steps, stood up, and came toward them, a dripping wet blur in her eyes, nicely tanned.

He reached for his towel laying across a bench and inclined his head in their direction. "Ladies," was all he said in greeting, then threw on a terry cloth robe and left before either one of them could reply.

"Man of few words," Jenna commented as they shed

their wraps and dove into the pool. Verrick merely nodded and started swimming laps, she felt more stressed than usual this evening and set about working out the tension and stiffness.

She felt invigorated when they stepped out of the pool.

"You were wrong. He doesn't have any."

"Have any what?"

"Tattoos or body piercings."

"I hadn't noticed."

"Verrick, that man has a body to notice—long, lean, and everything in perfect order."

"I told you he was perfect." As they walked toward the elevator she added, to emphasise her point, "He doesn't even sweat."

"Everyone sweats."

"He doesn't."

Jenna giggled and looked at her friend curiously, waiting for further explanation.

"I bumped into him out jogging, literally bumped into him—collided. I was all sweaty, damp hair, wet patches on my T-shirt, out of breath, and smelling like an old running shoe."

"Sounds like you."

Verrick stepped into the elevator and pressed the fourth floor. "You should have seen him—direct from a page in *Gentleman's Quarterly*. Every hair was in place, his shirt was dry, smelling of spring breeze, and he wasn't out of breath. And I swear, not a glimmer of perspiration."

The two women walked to Verrick's door and she fished the key out of her pocket. "I tell you, Jenna, the man doesn't sweat."

"Does he go to the bathroom?"

"I've never seen it." Verrick closed the door behind them. "If he does, it's likely only to adjust his halo."

After dinner, they did a thorough grocery shop in readiness for Thanksgiving—cranberries, brussel sprouts, bread for stuffing the turkey, and enough food to feed a dozen people.

Verrick pulled her car up outside the entrance to Westerly Place and they unloaded all the grocery bags into the lobby, before parking in the underground lot. There were more bags than the two women could carry in one trip. But that problem was solved.

As they stood in front of the open elevator, looking at the mountain of groceries, a man about their age, dressed in blue jeans and a turtleneck sweater, came in through the grand entrance doors. He took in their predicament at a glance, flashed a beautiful set of white teeth, picked up the grocery bags remaining on the floor, and followed them into the elevator.

From behind arms filled with grocery bags, a stalk of celery partially obscuring her face, Verrick managed a polite, "Thank you."

The man smiled easily. "My pleasure."

He walked beside Jenna to Verrick's door, where she had to deposit her load onto the carpet before inserting the key. He was very much a gentleman, arranged the bags carefully on the kitchen counters, then gathered the last bag from the hallway.

Either he was a very cheerful person or he was amused by something. He extended his hand to Verrick and introduced himself, "Gavin Parford."

Automatically, she took his hand and replied, "Verrick Grant."

Jenna couldn't hold back. "There's more than one?"

Gavin Parford didn't have any trouble guessing her meaning. "Oh, you must have met my older brother. Lion can be a bit intimidating, can't he?"

Neither Jenna nor Verrick needed to answer. Their grins said it all.

"Once you get to know him, Lion is really a lamb."

Verrick choked on that thought. "I'll take your word for it, Mr. Parford. Thanks again for your help."

He left with a casual wave and a friendly, "Happy Thanksgiving."

They didn't see his smug look of triumph as he headed to the other penthouse apartment.

I know something Lion doesn't. Her name is Verrick.

The morning sun had begun to brighten the lemon-yellow walls of Verrick's kitchen when she started stuffing the enormous turkey. Over twenty pounds, the bird had to be in the oven early if they planned to eat at six o'clock. Nothing was worse than undercooked turkey, still pink at the bones. She had the cranberry sauce cooked and all her platters and serving dishes down from the top shelves. Now she could relax for the day and welcome friends to her new home.

The same scene was playing out fifty miles away in the Parford home, only it was the family cook putting the turkey in the oven, and the east-facing kitchen was in a substantial mansion on a half-acre of manicured grounds. The cranberry sauce was cooked here, too, and the platters and serving dishes were sparkling after a fresh washing. Preparations were well under way for the fifteen members of the Parford family to sit down together for Thanksgiving dinner.

Mrs. Parford was the first to appear in the kitchen. She was a striking woman of Swedish descent, her blond hair going gracefully gray and her Nordic complexion aging naturally with laugh lines, the humor reflected in her sparkling blue eyes.

"Good morning, Birgit. Are you ready for the starving hordes?"

"Yes, ma'am, the bird's in the oven."

"Come join me for breakfast. It's a long day for you to be on your feet."

The two older women, both in their sixties, sat down at the kitchen table to eat fresh fruit with yogurt, bran muffins and several cups of coffee. Together, they had watched the

Parford's five children grow up, three of them now married, five grandchildren already and Rachel expecting her first child near Christmas. Only the eldest and youngest sons were still single.

"I have some nice chrysanthemums in the garden. I'll cut those for the dining room, shall I? I'll set the table too, so you won't have to give it another thought."

"That'll be nice, ma'am. I'll sit with my feet up for a spell this morning. Things will be jumping once the troops begin to arrive."

Sonya Parford agreed. "But it's lovely having them all home for Thanksgiving, isn't it?"

"Just so long as they leave at the end of the day."

The elderly cook loved every one of the Parford children as much as their mother, but she kept up a pretense of being gruff and ill-tempered. No good comes of spoiling a child.

Mrs. Parford, an avid gardener, took a stroll through her beloved garden, clipping armloads of chrysanthemums in shades of bronze, russet and yellow. Forty years they'd lived in this same house, since the day she was married. She carried the flowers into her greenhouse to trim the stems and pluck off some of the lower leaves. As each child was born, they came home to this very same house, first Lionel, then Martin and Alice and finally, the twins, Rachel and Gavin. Had it really been thirty-eight years since that day they brought their first son home from the hospital with his mane of blonde hair like her own and deep brown eyes like his father's? She shook the dew off the flowers and carried them into the house to arrange.

Douglas should be up by now, she'd join him for another cup of coffee. The morning quiet would be disrupted with voices before long.

The gathering of the Parfords was a happy celebration, lively with children's voices mixed in amongst the adults'. When Alice arrived with her two-year-old twins, the noise level went up several notches.

Sonya Parford was chatting with her eldest son. "Take

the twins outside for a while, would you, dear? Alice looks like she needs a breather."

Lionel gathered up his bouncing nephews and herded them out to the sandbox, swings and climbing gym in the yard. He knew the routine. He'd done it often enough with his younger brothers and sisters. Give them a good workout, plenty of fresh air and exercise, and they would be able to sit through dinner without fussing and squirming.

The two-year-olds chortled and squealed as their uncle pushed them on the swings and showed them how to dig tunnels in the sand.

The ploy worked. The children were quiet and biddable when the family sat down to watch Douglas Parford carve the Thanksgiving turkey.

Although she would never let on, Birgit was pleased to see the food disappear. Like a swarm of locusts, she described the Parford clan descending on a meal.

Rachel, very much pregnant, ate enough for two, even though she moaned about the amount of weight she'd gained.

"You're sure it's not twins?" her sister asked.

"Definitely not. George and I both saw the scan. We are having only one child at a time."

"Well, you're big enough to be carrying twins."

She glowered at her twin brother.

"Don't worry, dear," Martin consoled her. "You know what they say about large women . . ."

All three brothers answered in chorus, "Warm in winter, shade in summer."

Everyone around the table laughed, even Rachel.

"Lionel, how is life in the retirement capital? Are all the gray-haired ladies knitting you socks and baking you cookies?"

"I haven't received a single pair of socks or any cookies yet."

"These things take time."

"Now, now," Mrs. Parford refereed. "White Rock isn't

all elderly people. I'm sure there are plenty of young families there, too."

"You're right, Mother. There's a babe living next door to Lion."

A chorus of "ooh's and aah's" greeted that piece of information.

"Are we to expect an announcement soon?" Rachel asked suggestively.

Lionel's regal bearing went unchanged. He'd suffered his siblings' teasing for so long, he'd grown to expect it. Gavin answered for him.

"Lion's getting long in the tooth. He told me he doesn't pounce on just anything that crosses his path."

"Now, children, your brother isn't that old."

"He's ancient, Mother. Look how he's joined the gray-haired set to watch the tide come in and go out. That's the height of excitement at Westerly Place. It's a retirement home."

Douglas Parford joined the conversation at this point. "What's this I hear about it being nominated for a design award?"

"Yes, the selection committee toured it a few days ago. They seemed impressed."

Lionel well remembered showing the judges around, pointing out structural details, the state-of-the-art heating system and the creative use of materials. He dreaded the moment they asked to see through the second top floor suite. The last time he'd seen it, the smoke alarm was ringing and the place looked stirred with a stick. It wouldn't impress the judges.

He was pleasantly surprised.

Not only did its owner clean up well, she'd done wonders with the living space. The judges were highly impressed with the very feminine feel, so different from his. The woman had some beautiful pieces and a fine eye for color. She could be an interior decorator, the decor looked professional yet lived in. Miss Grant was not as disorganized as his first impression led him to believe. She was a woman full of surprises.

His father's voice pulled him back into the conversation. "Good for you, son."

At the same time, a successful Thanksgiving celebration was winding down on the top floor of Westerly Place, old friends gathered to share the holiday. True to her word, Jenna had baked pumpkin pies and her boyfriend, Ralph, had provided vast quantities of whipped cream. Darren brought wine, and several guests brought flowers, chrysanthemums in harvest shades exactly the same as those decorating the Parford home.

Everyone had suggestions for the starlight ballroom.

"It looks like a bowling alley."

"No, shuffleboard. It looks like a ship's deck."

"I say it should have mirrors along the inside wall, and a barre and it would be a dance studio."

"No. It should have incense candles burning and mats on the floor for yoga and meditation."

"It's an artist's studio, great light. All it needs is an easel."

"A home for reptiles, snakes, iguanas. They love the heat."

"What are your plans, Verrick?"

"My first thought was plants, but I'm a klutz at growing things."

"Use plastic plants. They don't need any care, they don't die or get pests, and they look almost real."

The guests left, having eaten more than anyone intended, in twos and threes, sharing the drive back into Vancouver.

The dishes were washed and put away, the last of the turkey in the refrigerator, and the last of the wine in the glasses that Ralph, Jenna and Darren lifted in a toast to Verrick's happiness in her new home.

Jenna produced a bulky package. "A housewarming gift."

The card said, "To Verrick, something to share your empty bed." Verrick raised eyebrows, wondering what her friend was up to. She undid the wrapping and laughed at the sight of a large, golden stuffed lion, with a full blonde mane and dark brown eyes.

"Company for you," Jenna teased.

Verrick lifted the majestic lion with its proud bearing, and looked it over from all sides. "It has the right attitude."

She grinned at her friend. "Thank you . . . I think."

When Lionel Parford drove past the well-lit front of Westerly Place to the parking entrance, he spotted the Mercedes parked at the curb. He looked up to the fourth floor and could see lights still on, then down at his watch— almost midnight. Wasn't it time the guy went home?

He parked his car and walked up the four flights of stairs to his own door, not wanting to meet the owner of the Mercedes, or anyone else, in the elevator.

He'd spent a lovely day with his family, but something was irritating him.

As Gavin put it, "I'll stick a thorn in the Lion's paw."

The two brothers left their parents' home together, each going to their separate cars. As they unlocked their driver's side doors, Gavin called out that final barb.

"Her name is Verrick."

He knew he'd struck the mark, when the silver Porsche shot out of the driveway with a burst of speed. And he saw the growl on Lion's face.

Chapter Three

Mr. Stephenson was waiting to corner Verrick when she returned from work Tuesday evening.

"Wonderful news, Miss Grant. Westerly Place has won the architectural design award. The residents are planning a potluck supper to celebrate Friday evening. Will you be able to come?"

"Of course, Mr. Stephenson. I wouldn't dream of missing it. Is there something special I should bring? We can't have everyone bringing potato salad."

"My wife knows more about that than I do. I'll have her give you a call."

Verrick swam her laps in peace that evening, mulling over the award. The architect truly did deserve it. She hadn't found a flaw in Westerly Place yet. Everything had been considered, it was a lovely place to live—perfect, in fact.

As she splashed in a leisurely pace back and forth across the pool, she wondered if the architect would attend the celebration. She'd like to meet him. He'd done an excellent job. He knew all the tiny considerations that made a house a home.

Mrs. Stephenson had suggested she bring a dessert. She

thought about appropriate recipes as she rubbed her hair dry. Chocolate cake, she decided—everybody eats chocolate cake. She'd bake one on Thursday and have it iced and ready for Friday.

There was quite a crowd in the community room Friday evening. Most of her neighbors Verrick had already met, but tonight they were dressed for the occasion. Diamond earrings sparkled, precious necklaces gleamed, bracelets tinkled, and mascara, rouge and eye shadow glowed from elderly faces she'd only seen before with the barest traces of lipstick.

She was glad she'd taken time to dress with care. Her neighbors were setting a dress code hard to live up to. With one exception.

Mr. Parford towered above every other head in the room, resplendent in a perfectly-fitted suit of charcoal gray. The beige of his shirt accented the brown of his eyes, and his neatly-styled blonde hair shimmered in the subdued lighting.

His dress code was not hard to live up to; it was impossible.

Look at that hair—natural blonde of course, right to the scalp. I could be blonde too, if I wanted, she consoled herself. But her inner voice answered back. But you would have dark roots.

She gritted her teeth. *It's not fair.*

She watched him chatting up the elderly residents of the building. Just look at his eyelashes—thick, dark, fully an inch long. With three coats of mascara, mine couldn't look as good as that.

He saw her across the room, patiently listening to a talkative couple who lived on the first floor. She wasn't wearing glasses this evening. She looked great—like a natural flower amongst all the gilded lilies.

Mrs. Stephenson led Verrick off to see the plaque to be unveiled by the main entrance. It was covered at the moment, but the manager's wife told her it was engraved in silver with the architect's name, the date, and the title of the prestigious award.

She was appropriately impressed and looked about the room, wondering which one of the men in suits was the architect.

There wasn't time to study every face, as the guests began helping themselves from the lovely selections on the buffet table. There was *no* potato salad. Everyone had pulled out their most impressive recipe and spent days in the preparation.

Verrick especially enjoyed an unusual looking Thai curry with some ingredients she couldn't identify, but she tasted coconut milk and lemongrass.

"That's a lovely dish, isn't it, dear?"

"Delightful."

"Mr. Parford is so talented." Her eyes widened at the donor of the exotic dish. "He's widely traveled, you know. He brings back recipes from all corners of the world."

As if hearing his name from across the room, Mr. Parford looked over the heads of his dinner companions into those shockingly blue eyes. She was staring straight at him. He lifted his glass in silent acknowledgment and continued the conversation around his table.

The man probably ordered the dish from some Asian restaurant. She knew she was being mean-spirited. But did the man have to be so good at everything?

Listening to the people around her singing his praises, she vowed that one day she would find something that man wasn't perfect at. And she'd shout it from the rooftops.

The marvels of her neighbor were not laid to rest yet.

After a little speech praising Westerly Place, the plaque was unveiled amidst a spontaneous round of applause. Then Mr. Parford made an acceptance speech, Verrick figured on behalf of the residents, before everyone toasted the fine structure and went off to devour the offerings of the dessert table.

Verrick was amazed, although she should have been prepared for it, when she took a close look at the dedication plaque.

There, engraved in silver, mounted on polished mahogany, was the first line. Architect: Lionel Parford.

Of course, she muttered later, to herself, carrying her empty cake plate to her apartment, I should have known, there's nothing the man can't do.

Later that night, she related the whole affair to Jenna.

"He brought this sensational curry, nutritious, attractive, and wonderful tasting. Get this, he cooked it himself from a recipe he picked up in Thailand."

"What did you take?"

"I'm almost embarrassed to admit . . . a plain chocolate cake."

"You make great chocolate cake."

"It's no competition for splendiferous foreign cuisine. Think about it, Jenna—high calories, nutritionally unsound, sugar, fat, and chocolate—all bad for you, and everyone can bake a chocolate cake."

"But it tastes good."

"That's no excuse."

"If all the residents were at this dinner, did you find out if he's married?"

"Do you mean, is there a Mrs. Perfect?"

"That's what I'm asking."

"I didn't see her. But then . . . who knows . . . she's likely off cooking meals for the homeless."

Jenna chuckled as Verrick repeated once more, "That man makes me feel like a klutz."

"But you're not a klutz."

"Well, around him I sure feel like one. It's the strangest thing—my mind goes blank, my feet trip over themselves and my tongue gets too tangled to get out even the simplest phrase."

Jenna grinned. Her friend had it bad.

* * *

Halloween was fast approaching. There was the costume ball the hospital sponsored to raise money for much-needed equipment, and the visit to the children's ward. Verrick's costume was ready. It glittered and sparkled and made the people in her office grin like lunatics when she modeled it for them.

"It's you, Dr. Grant. Exactly right . . . a dentist dressing as the tooth fairy."

"I like the silver slippers."

"The magic wand and wings are the best."

"No, it's the glitsy crown. Wherever did you find such a thing?"

"Oh, this old thing. Doesn't every fairy have one in her closet?" Verrick's voice had changed, along with her mannerisms. She was on familiar ground, role playing.

"The children will love it."

"Yes, but who at the hospital ball will dance with a fairy? What man is brave enough to risk his reputation?"

Peals of laughter echoed through the office as Verrick fluttered off on her silver slippers.

The costume ball wasn't until later, but she was due to visit the children's ward in the afternoon, so they wouldn't be too excited to eat their dinners and settle for the night.

Verrick loved working with children, they were so open and unassuming. And they believed in fairies.

She was in full costume when she hurried to the elevator, a fantasy in silver and white, with rosy painted cheeks and outrageous glittery glasses. Her head was down as she checked to see her gossamer gown wasn't clinging to her underskirt or riding up around her knees.

The elevator doors opened before she had a chance to press the down button. She lifted her head to see her neighbor staring in awestruck silence. Immediately, she was in character.

She waved her magic wand and twittered, "Hello, Lionel."

That was the first time she'd called him by name. He hadn't realized she knew it. He decided to play along. She looked so ridiculous—enchanting, but ridiculous. "Hello. Have we met?"

"Oh my, yes." She batted her false eyelashes and jigged about on her silver slippers.

"Pardon me for not remembering."

"No pardon is necessary. Of course you wouldn't remember me. I only visit when good boys and girls are asleep in their beds." Her voice was bright and sing-songy.

"And why is that?"

"Oh, Lionel. Fairies are magic. You mustn't see them doing their work."

"Then how does anyone know you've been there?" He couldn't believe he was having this conversation. And with a fairy, no less.

"Dear boy, think. You put your tooth under your pillow and in the morning it's gone. In its place is a treat. Didn't you know I had come?"

A light was beginning to dawn. "Then I take it, you're the tooth fairy."

Verrick jumped up and down and clapped her hands together. "Lionel, you're such a clever boy."

She slipped through the open elevator doors, waggled her magic wand and called in a syrupy sweet voice, "Ta ta." The doors swished shut and she was gone.

His sides shook with laughter as he was left staring at the closed doors behind which the fairy had vanished.

The woman's a riot.

Either she belongs on the stage, or in an asylum.

The children were delighted with a visit from the tooth fairy. The Halloween party was a brilliant success. Balloons, party hats, a jack-o-lantern, and lots of paper ghosts and black cats, made up for anything the hospitalized children missed if they'd been well enough to go trick or treating.

Verrick enjoyed it, too.

Smiling children did her heart good.

The nurses on the ward thanked her profusely as she left with the rest of the party troupe.

Verrick felt that was backwards. She should thank them for making her welcome to share Halloween with the children.

In her childhood, Halloween was spent at boarding school—no parents fussing over a costume, no familiar neighborhood to go to. For that matter, no home to go to.

She shook her silver crown, excessive with false jewels, and scurried to her car. Her arrival would be a little late at the charity ball, but then, fairies were never expected to stick to rigid schedules.

The hospital ball was splendid. The room was decorated in orange and black streamers, corn stalks and sheaves of wheat as well as the ghosts and black cats like those on the children's ward. Candles flickered from inside ghoulish carved pumpkins. The blood-red punch had a severed hand floating in it (ice frozen in a rubber glove floated deathly-white in the bowl). Witches and goblins abounded. Verrick was in her element.

Lionel Parford watched her circulating through the crowd, she was well-known to many of the patrons here, and well-liked, judging from the number of hugs and kisses she received.

She really was a sight—as natural in that ridiculous outfit as if she wore it every day. She had the joyful ability of an innocent child to play-act and make those around her share her light-hearted humor. She sparkled through the room like sunshine and laughter.

The live band was playing a wide selection of music, some for the older guests and some for the younger ones. Lionel dutifully danced with doctors' wives and society matrons, catching glimpses of the tooth fairy and the men she was dancing with.

In costume, many people stepped out of their everyday

roles, becoming bolder and more daring. Young women he'd never met, some in very revealing outfits, insisted he dance, all the while flirting most obviously.

He kept telling himself this was for a worthy cause, raising money for the hospital, but he still had doubts about dressing as Prince Charming.

The scene in the costume rental shop was hard to forget.

The sales clerk first showed him superhero outfits—Superman, Batman and Spiderman.

He dismissed those instantly. "I refuse to wear tights."

"But sir, you have the physique to carry it off."

"No tights. That's final."

"Then perhaps the Prince Charming outfit? The pants are snug but there are high boots and a jerkin that comes below the hips . . . and covers . . ." He cleared his throat uncomfortably. ". . . if you know what I mean."

"I know what you mean." The poor sales clerk was cringing under the man's sharp tongue. Anyone else with the lean athletic body this customer had would be delighted to flaunt it in a skin tight costume.

He looked down at his own protruding belly, hanging over his belt. He knew he would flaunt it, if he were in half the shape this tall Viking was.

Lionel tried on the outfit; it was the least revealing of all the ones shown him.

"Which of the headdresses would you prefer, this plumed hat, or the gold crown?"

The scorching look the green velvet cap with the fluffy ostrich plume received, should have reduced it to ashes.

"Perhaps the crown," the astute sales clerk offered, "appropriate but understated."

Lionel allowed it to be placed on his striking blonde head. He wasn't pleased, but it would do.

The humiliations he put himself through to fulfill his civic duty and donate to a worthy cause. It would be easier to put a check in the mail and be done with it.

The red-haired vixen he was dancing with didn't share that opinion. Prince Charming was an excellent dancer any girl would be proud to catch. *He must be new to White Rock, I would have noticed anyone looking this good if he'd been around long.*

He returned his dance partner to her table and sat down with a resigned sigh beside several members of the hospital board at his own table.

An elderly doctor patted him on the shoulder. "Quite the ladies' man, Parford."

"Hardly. I got railroaded into this. I drew up the blueprints for the new hospice facility and every person I've met since has insisted I attend the Halloween Ball."

The elderly gentlemen and their wives chuckled.

"You've missed one."

"Missed one what?"

"You've missed dancing with one of the lovely young ladies."

Lionel could have sworn he'd danced with every female in the room, been ogled, drooled over, and ravaged with their hungry eyes. He'd had quite enough.

Politely he smiled and disagreed. "You must be mistaken."

"Oh no, you haven't danced with the sugar plum fairy."

Lionel turned and scanned the dance floor. "That's not the sugar plum fairy, that's the tooth fairy."

There was gentle laughter around the table.

"That familiar with fairies, are you, Parford?"

He could laugh at himself about that. "You've got me there."

"Better remedy the situation, before the girl vanishes in a puff of smoke."

With the half dozen pairs of eyes focussed on him, he couldn't wriggle out of one more dance. "It's for charity," he silently reminded himself.

He excused himself from the table and sought out the

fairy. She was standing at the edge of the dance floor, thanking a young doctor who was staring at her with a bedazzled look.

She saw him coming.

He bowed majestically before her. "May I have this dance?"

She sparkled up at him, curtsying most graciously. "Why Prince Charming, I'd be delighted." She took her leave of the young doctor and accepted Lionel's hand as he led her onto the dance floor.

They made an eye-catching couple, he so tall and blonde, and she, sparkling in silver. The band struck up an old-fashioned waltz, most fitting for Prince Charming and the belle of the ball.

The newspaper photographers present thought so, too. They followed the couple, lenses focused, flashbulbs ready.

She fit into his arms as light and airy as a make-believe fairy should. But she wasn't make-believe. She was real and soft and warm to his touch, and she danced effortlessly, graceful and demure in her silver slippers.

His experience with fairies was limited, but he expected her to smell of sulphur and smoke, bitter potions, and sneezy fairy dust. She didn't. She smelled glorious. The fragrance of lilacs, sweet and sumptuous on a spring breeze, enfolded him. He dipped his head closer to her lightly scented hair and inhaled deeply, a blissful look of enchantment on his handsome face with half-closed eyes.

That was when the photographers snapped their pictures.

The couple was quite unaware, waltzing to the lovely music, content in each other's arms, caught up in the moment, with no need for speech.

When the music finished, it seemed too soon. He was loathe to release her.

"May I offer you a ride home?"

"I came in my own car."

"I'd feel better if I accompanied you home. I could follow in my car." He smiled with all the charm a storybook prince should have. "It isn't safe to be loose on the streets dressed like that."

She looked him over slowly from gold crown, to braided jerkin, skin-tight pants, and down to polished knee boots. "You're in danger yourself, sweet prince."

She whispered it softly, suggestively, almost enough to make him blush.

He admitted her point, but refused defeat. "I'll walk you to your car."

"Thank you," she twinkled as she curtsied. "You may need my protection."

She crossed the room to join a group of friends she had eaten dinner with.

Costume balls weren't so bad after all.

He was true to his word and accompanied her to her car, then drove slowly behind her all the way to Westerly Place. They locked their respective cars, then with his hand at her back he guided her to the elevator and stood silently beside her as it whisked them up four floors.

At this early morning hour, she still looked radiant, and the essence of lilacs fleetingly teased his nostrils. He'd always loved lilacs.

She expected him to turn to his own apartment once out of the elevator, but he walked her to her door. She'd left her key under the mat and bent to pick it up. His large hand covered hers and he gallantly found the key and unlocked her door.

There was a moment of tension . . . hesitation at parting . . . uncertainty about how you say goodnight to a vision.

Verrick took the initiative. When playing a role, she was confident and sure of herself. She stood on tiptoe and kissed him gently on the cheek. "Good night, sweet prince."

He couldn't leave her like that. He drew her firmly into his arms, so close against his chest she could feel his heart beating, lowered his head and kissed her properly—if a long, sensuous, heart-wrenching kiss could be considered proper.

He was more in control than she was when he released her, but only slightly. She wasn't sure her knees wouldn't buckle. He was still standing and took a step backward.

"Good night, Verrick."

It took all his shattered composure to turn and walk the length of the hallway to the door of his own apartment.

Dazed, Verrick stepped through her door, closed it softly behind her, then leaned her back up against it.

That kiss wasn't make-believe. He wasn't pretending. He called her Verrick.

She left a trail of discarded clothing on the way to her bedroom, magic wand, gossamer wings, jewelled crown, silver slippers, glittering gown, swirling underskirt, and finally her own brief underwear. She washed quickly and slipped beneath her sheets, exhausted and ready for sleep.

Her last waking thought was, "That man's kiss was perfection."

The morning paper was full of it, colored front page photo and large print headline: PRINCE CHARMING DANCES WITH FAIRY. The photographer had caught Lionel Parford's look of enchantment as he held Verrick in his arms. The accompanying text told about the hospital ball and made insinuating remarks about Prince Charming being bewitched and under the spell of the enticing fairy.

Miles away, Gavin Parford caught sight of the photo and hooted with laughter. Immediately he procured the negative, had it blown up to poster size and gave one to his parents and each of his siblings.

Sonya Parford accepted the poster and remarked, "Don't they look charming."

Her youngest son was beside himself with glee at finding something to tease his older brother about. "Look at Lionel. He's positively swooning."

"Lionel doesn't swoon, dear." She smiled at Gavin gloating over the picture. "He looks . . . happy."

"Mother, he looks spellbound."

"It was a costume ball, dear. You can't expect Lion to look as sober as he usually does."

"This is priceless. Good old poker-faced Lion looks stricken."

Mrs. Parford was looking closely at the picture. "I'll show this to Birgit. Perhaps we'll hang it in the kitchen."

She had to admit, her eldest son looked blissful. She wondered who the girl was. She'd like to meet her.

It took weeks for Lionel Parford to live down that photograph. Thanks to Gavin, he found it larger than life, hanging prominently in his friends' homes, in his office, on the walls of his sisters' living rooms, even his mother had one hanging in her kitchen.

That was the last time he'd dance with a fairy in public.

Mrs. Parford didn't have to wait long to meet the mystery girl in the photograph.

On Saturday morning, Verrick pulled a heavy blue sweater over her head, zipped up her jeans, tied the laces on her comfortable walking shoes, and set off for a browse through the antique shops on Marine Drive her office receptionist had recommended. There wasn't anything she really needed, but she hadn't explored her new neighborhood and treasures turned up when you least expected.

In the entrance lobby, a woman was poring over a street map of White Rock, obviously in need of directions. She was an older woman, perhaps in her sixties, with a genuine warmth and friendliness in her smile. She must have been a beauty in her day, she still was, in Verrick's opinion. Her once blonde hair was attractively turning gray, her lovely face was unadorned with heavy makeup, false eyelashes, or brilliant red lipstick, and she was wearing the elegant sort of clothing appropriate to a woman her age—a tailored jacket over matching sweater and slacks. She was the image Verrick long wished her own mother would be. To no avail.

"Can I help?"

"Yes. I'm a little disoriented."

"What address were you looking for?"

"Oh, it wasn't an address exactly. My son told me about an antique shop within walking distance. I can't resist a good snoop through old things, they have such history, such rich memories of past owners."

That was exactly how Verrick felt.

"I'd be happy to show you the way. I'm going in that direction myself."

"That would be lovely. You're sure it's no trouble?"

Verrick held the door open and the two women stepped out onto the sidewalk. There was a nip in the air but the sky was clear and the November sunshine added its warmth as they walked briskly along Marine Drive, past a book store, souvenir shops, restaurants, and all manner of clothing stores. Both women were new to White Rock and stopped frequently to admire things in store windows— Indian carvings, smoked salmon packaged as souvenirs, and maple syrup in tiny decorative bottles. They window-shopped happily together, as if they'd known each other for ages.

"Have you just moved into Westerly Place?"

"Heavens no, dear. My husband and I are visiting our son for the weekend. Douglas has no patience for antiques, he calls them all dusty secondhand junk." She was chattering away to this young woman as if they were familiar old friends. Not surprising, since she saw her picture every day, in full living color, hanging in the kitchen.

"Where are my manners? Forgive me, dear. I'm Sonya Parford." She extended her hand as if there were no need for introductions. Strangely, Verrick already felt she had so much in common with this woman.

"Verrick Grant. Pleased to meet you, Mrs. Parford."

The older woman smiled approval. The young lady knew

her manners, no first name basis for the elderly, very respectful. No wonder Lionel had that dazed look in the photo.

She was a rare find in these modern times.

"Verrick, where were you all day? I phoned several times and kept getting your answering machine.

"I checked out the shops along Marine Drive."

"By yourself?"

"No, I ran into Mr. Parford's mother . . ."

"You're kidding!"

"I'm serious, Jenna. You'll never guess what she's like."

"Perfect. Right?"

"You guessed it, first try . . . the sort of mother who is kind, nurturing, loves children . . ."

It didn't take much for Jenna to fill in the unspoken words. "Everything Elly is not."

The line was silent for a moment, then Verrick quietly admitted the obvious. "Everything Elly is not," she agreed, a note of sadness making her voice husky.

"Did her son come, too?"

"No, he was out searching for antiquated books with his father. But his mother took me into his apartment for tea."

"What's it like inside? No don't tell me . . . let me guess. It's perfect."

Verrick laughed. "He isn't called Mr. Perfect for nothing. The place is splendid, big solid furnishings, impressive collectibles from his travels, lots of green and beige, masculine but not severe."

"Does he have a starlight ballroom?"

"Yes. You should see it—slate floor, a profusion of plants, and lounge furniture from some island he visited in the South Seas."

"Wicker?"

"No, bamboo and some other tropical woods. Wicker would probably mildew and rot; it was like a greenhouse in there."

"So, he's a horticultural whiz as well?"

"Mrs. Parford told me her son Gavin set it up, all computer controlled, windows that open and close for ventilation, sun shades that lower when the brightness index is too high and little spaghetti hoses to the base of every plant, automatically controlled to deliver water and nutrients exactly when needed. It was a marvel. I'd never seen anything like it."

"Did you find out any nasty bits about the man from his mother?"

"No. She hardly mentioned him. She was most gracious, we had a very genteel tea—fine bone china, cucumber sandwiches on paper thin bread and rich scones with whipped cream."

"He can't be that perfect. It isn't humanly possible. Everyone has faults and foibles."

"I've told you, Jenna. Scratch his perfect exterior and you find perfection underneath. Everything he puts his hand to turns out superior. Who could measure up to a person so flawless?"

Jenna heard her friend's unspoken doubt that the man could find anything in her to admire. Reassuringly, she said, "If you dig deep enough, you'll find dirt."

"Jenna, I'd be the one covered in dirt. He'd be immaculate. Tell me why you were trying to reach me all day. I don't want to hear another word about that man."

"The film shoot is scheduled for November eighteenth. I've gathered some great stuff from the props department and we're ready to fit out your starlight ballroom. Can we get into your building to set things up?"

"I'll leave a key with the manager." She paused and digested her friend's words. She detected a whiff of intrigue in Jenna's voice. "What kind of things?"

"Things to reveal his character, you know . . . gothic stuff . . . lots of black, antique fittings, things from an ancient lab. . . ."

"Aarrgh . . ." was the only sound that travelled down the telephone lines.

As pleasant memories of an elegant ladylike tea faded into contrasting visions of a weird horror-film doctor, Verrick apprehensively wondered what she'd gotten herself into.

Chapter Four

"Verrick, honey, where is this place you've moved to?"

"It's in White Rock, Mother, half an hour's drive south of Vancouver."

"Isn't that where old people get put out to pasture?"

"No, Mother. There is a retirement community . . . but horses get put out to pasture, not people."

"Whatever . . . why didn't you stay in Vancouver? That's where things are happening, lots of eligible men, plenty of great places to be seen. Why do you want to bury yourself out in the sticks? You'll never see any action."

"I like it here, Mother. My work is here and I'm not looking for action."

"Don't take that prissy tone with me. If anyone had told me a daughter of mine would turn out a bitter old maid, I wouldn't have believed it."

"We've been over this before, Mother . . ."

"And stop calling me Mother. It makes me sound like some dull old woman whose idea of fun is baking cookies."

"You're neither old nor dull, and you know it. Why are you phoning me?"

The petulant voice became sweet and syrupy. "Honey lamb, I wondered if I could stay with you for a few days."

"Did Arthur keep the townhouse in your latest divorce?"

"No, no, nothing like that. Arthur adores me, he wouldn't be so penny pinching."

"Then why do you need a place to stay?"

"I'm having a little hospital visit . . . and I'll need time to recover. I thought it would be an opportunity for us to spend time together."

"What is it this time, Mother, liposuction, a tummy tuck, another face lift?"

"You needn't be so nasty. A woman has to keep up appearances."

"I'm sorry, Mother. Which hospital will you be in?"

"Vancouver General."

"Give me the date and time and I'll be there to pick you up. I have a spare bedroom you're welcome to use as long as you like."

"I knew you'd see sense, honey, lamb. You always come around eventually."

When Verrick arrived in the hospital at the appointed time, her mother was dressed and waiting. The last time she'd seen Eloise Thornton, she had platinum blonde hair and a wealthy cattleman husband. As no surprise, the hair color had changed and she'd divorced the cattleman.

Her mother was a sight to behold. Her hair was flaming red, a color that didn't suit her natural coloring, but that wasn't a problem as nothing natural showed. She was never seen without makeup and today was no exception. Verrick long suspected her mother applied makeup with a spatula, her face was honey bronze, her cheeks creamy rose, her lips dazzling orchid, and her eyebrows dark sable. All those descriptive words had fascinated Verrick as she read them on her mother's cosmetics as a child. But she could see nothing more of her mother's face; an enormous pair of sunglasses covered not only her eyes but nearly half her face.

"Mother, it's November. You won't need the sunglasses."

"Honey lamb, one can never be too careful."

Verrick shrugged, helped her mother gather her things, dealt with her discharge, then carried the two large suitcases as a nurse wheeled her patient to the waiting car."

"Are you still driving this old thing? You can afford a decent car, why do you insist on driving this piece of junk?"

The nurse helped Verrick settle her mother into the passenger seat, a look of sympathy and the unspoken message, "Better you than me," passing between the two women. Verrick thanked her politely and slipped into the driver's seat.

Traffic was heavy, and for once Verrick was glad, it gave her an excuse to only nod or murmur in response to her mother's high-pitched conversation. Her ramblings were familiar, clothes and jewelry she'd bought, fascinating parties she'd attended, rich people she'd met, and lavish trips she'd taken. Eloise Thornton enjoyed everything money could buy.

But it couldn't buy her daughter's respect.

Over the years, Verrick had been embarrassed, bewildered, occasionally ashamed, and even mortified by her mother's values and behavior. School vacations she spent with her were invariably in a different location each time, quite often with a new husband and Verrick was thankful to return to the orderly, modest life at boarding school.

How a mother and daughter could be so different, puzzled everyone who came to know them.

While Verrick wrestled with two large suitcases and a heavy cosmetic case, Eloise Thornton waltzed into the entrance lobby of Westerly Place in her frilly fuschia ensemble tottering on dangerously high-heeled, open-toed shoes. She was assessing the merits of her daughter's new home, tasteful, reserved, and discreetly expensive—not her style, when from behind her dark glasses she spotted something that was definitely her style.

Like a light switch clicking on, her whole demeanor

changed. Her face lit up with an alluring smile, her body wriggled within the folds of her tight-fitting dress, and her hands fluttered girlishly in front of her face.

He was very much her style, tall, handsome, well-dressed and with deep pockets if he was in a place like this.

Her shrill voice vanished and in its place was the breathy whisper of a seductress. "Honey, you are just so big and strong . . ." Her painted nails (raspberry blush) curled around his forearm. "Could you help a damsel in distress with all this heavy luggage?" The fact that she was only carrying a handbag and Verrick was weighted down with her suitcases, didn't phase her one bit.

The object of her attentions had taken in the situation at a glance when he reached the top of the stairs from the parking garage. He was a master at chivalry. He smiled at the fawning woman, if you could call it a smile, the corners of his mouth turned up so slightly it was barely noticeable.

His deep voice gained an approving giggle from the woman clinging to his arm. "Allow me."

With that, he stepped over to Verrick, relieved her of the two large suitcases, pressed the elevator button, removed his arm from the raspberry blush claws and motioned for the two ladies to enter the elevator.

Eloise reattached herself to his arm the instant the doors swished shut. She was speaking to Verrick but didn't bother to turn her head to look at her; she was so busy studying the man reflected in the mirrored elevator wall. "Honey lamb, you must introduce me to this gorgeous man."

Verrick was to one side of her mother, patiently watching her in action. It wasn't anything new. In fact, she'd seen it so often, she didn't blush or feel embarrassed any more. She calmly looked up into the attentive brown eyes watching her and took care of the introductions in a matter-of-fact voice. "Lionel Parford, Eloise Thornton."

"Call me Elly," her mother trilled. "Everyone does."

The elevator reached the fourth floor and Lionel stood back to let the ladies precede him. Verrick, still lugging the heavy cosmetic case, stepped into the hallway but her mother stayed where she was, hanging on Lionel's arm. Verrick turned and gave him a look as if to say, "Nice try. You won't shake her off that easily."

He caught that look and blessed her with a warm, generous smile. For a moment she thought he understood and sympathized.

But that was impossible. With a dignified mother like his, he had no idea how irritating a mother like Elly Thornton could be.

She reached her door first, unlocked it, and gestured for her mother to enter. But Elly wasn't letting go of her captive just yet. "Lionel . . . you don't mind me calling you Lionel, do you?" He didn't answer; he was watching Verrick. Her face was so expressive. He could almost guess her thoughts.

She was thinking, "Be thankful for small mercies. She could have decided to call you sweetie pie or sugar dumpling."

Elly was oblivious to the wordless communication passing between the other two people in the doorway. "Lionel, honey, you will join us for dinner, won't you?"

Verrick gagged. Elly couldn't boil water. What was she planning to serve the man?

Lionel Parford came up with the perfect response. "I'd be delighted to have dinner with two such lovely ladies." Elly pouted at the idea of sharing him with anyone, but he didn't give her a chance to interrupt. "But I couldn't forgive myself if I was the cause of you toiling over a hot stove. It would be my pleasure to take you both out to dinner. Would seven o'clock be convenient?"

He was good. He handled Elly so smoothly and with such practiced skill, he must have women throwing themselves at his feet on a regular basis.

Elly was preening, like a peacock with its tail feathers spread for all to see. Not ten minutes in the building, and she had a dinner invitation with this sexy hunk. "Lionel, sugar, you are just too perfect."

"Oh, if only you knew," Verrick groaned silently within.

He disengaged Elly's clinging hand and gave her a gentle nudge toward Verrick's living room.

His eyes were consumed by the lovely woman so quietly accepting her guest's behavior. Her natural beauty was made greater in contrast with the painted woman wobbling on excessively high heels to check out Verrick's new home.

His voice was tender. "Will seven o'clock be convenient for you?" There was a wealth of perception in those few repeated words. He was asking if she was all right, if she could handle this woman in her life, if he could help by taking them out for dinner. He was asking her to trust him.

She smiled, some recognition of all that was left unsaid in her soft voice. "Thank you."

He couldn't resist. A weariness, a forlorn sadness, made her seem so vulnerable. He lowered his head and kissed her.

Her cornflower blue eyes were wide, staring up at him, as he closed the door and walked to his apartment.

The tooth fairy took more than teeth. She took a man's senses as well.

Elly Thornton wasn't admiring the spectacular sea view or resting in one of the inviting armchairs when Verrick joined her in the living room. She had removed her over-sized dark glasses and was up close, peering into the oak-framed mirror over the bookcase.

"Good Lord! What have you done to yourself?"

She turned to face her daughter. Both eyes were blood-shot, the area around them swollen in shades from red through blue to black.

"You're such a worrier. It's nothing . . . a little tightening up, eliminating that ugly baggy skin under my eyes."

"Is it painful?"

With her dark glasses firmly back in place, she shrugged. "The doctor gave me something for that."

"Mother, it looks terrible."

"Honey lamb, stop fussing. A girl has to take care of her appearance. If a little discomfort here and there is what it takes, it's worth it." She looked around the spacious room, not interested in its unique design or tasteful furnishings. "Which way to my bedroom? I'll have to redo my makeup and change before that luscious man comes to take us to dinner."

Verrick led her to the guest room and the question she was expecting wasn't long in coming. "You wouldn't have other plans for this evening, would you, sweetie pie?"

"No, Mother." She knew her mother's tactics and she wasn't willing to play along. Mr. Parford had been more than neighborly, inviting them to dine. She wasn't going to unleash Eloise Thornton on him unchaperoned. She had to live in the same building with the man, how could she face him after putting him through an evening of fending off Elly as she pawed and drooled over him? "I had no plans, Mother. I was expecting you, remember?"

Elly was disgruntled but her daughter posed no competition when it came to attracting a man. *Look at her—almost thirty and not married even once. Why, at that age I was looking for my third husband.* As Verrick carried her suitcases into the charming room, her mother began unpacking, spreading filmy dresses and a bounty of accessories over the delicate quilt covering the bed. Verrick began putting them on hangers and arranging them in the closet. There was an awful lot of pink.

"What about this Darryl you've been seeing . . . ?"

"His name is Darren, Mother."

"Darren, Darryl, whatever. He's making good money, drives a nice car, what are you waiting for? Why haven't you married him?"

"Marriage isn't high on my list of things to do, Mother. I'm happy as I am, I like my work, I enjoy my friends . . ."

"It's not normal."

"Between you and father, I've witnessed seven marriages close up, none of them lasting. I don't want to put myself through that kind of heartbreak and misery."

"It's not misery, Honey lamb, it's fun while it lasts."

Her mother's ability to bounce back after a failed relationship amazed Verrick. Here she was, barely divorced two weeks, on the prowl for husband number six. She didn't lose faith in marriage. Perhaps if she tried it often enough, she'd get it right.

Verrick was optimistic but not when it came to marriage. The word terrified her.

She left her mother to get ready for dining out. From long experience, she knew the colossal amount of time achieving "the right look" took. She could cook dinner, tidy the kitchen, and read the better part of a novel, in the time her mother took to get ready.

She welcomed the chance to unwind. Elly hadn't changed, still the girlish, boy-crazy woman she'd always been. Verrick felt the roles had been reversed, she was the conservative, sensible mother to Elly, the rebellious, acting-out child. She made herself a cup of tea and dreaded the evening to follow.

At exactly seven o'clock, there was a knock on the door. Of course, Verrick answered it. Elly was still in her bedroom.

Verrick couldn't imagine how he did it. He was dressed exactly right, every hair in place, his clothes immaculate, and a calm unruffled expression on his face. If she wasn't mistaken, he found this all rather amusing.

He didn't say any such thing but the grooves at the side of his mouth and the arch of his eyebrows made her smile in return.

Elly would be as outrageous as she always was. There was nothing Verrick could do about it, so she might as well relax and make the best of it. It was like being on a toboggan ride; once you push off you have to ride it to the bottom, no matter how fast or how scary.

When Lionel Parford smiled at her like that, she felt the ride was pushed off and picking up speed.

"Good evening." He looked around for the woman who gave him an excuse to invite Verrick for dinner. "I hope I'm not too early."

"No, no. You're exactly on time." She was grappling for words to explain. "Elly is . . . she doesn't . . . she prefers a grand entrance, usually late."

He didn't seem to mind. Actually he'd expected it and made dinner reservations for eight o'clock.

"Would you like a drink while we're waiting?"

"Only if you're having one."

"Don't let me stop you. I'm not much of a drinker . . . designated driver . . . and all that."

"Then I won't either as I'm the one driving this evening." He imagined her abstinence had something to do with Elly's overindulgence. Just as her minimum of makeup, jewelry, and provocative clothing was probably in reaction to the other woman's lavish use. She was beautiful, simply dressed in a soft blue dress, very proper but it clung in all the right places. Her glasses were absent today, all the better to see her lovely eyes. They shone out at him from that poster Gavin had put in his office but they were even lovelier up close.

Elly chose that moment to sashay in. She wasn't going to leave that handsome man cooling his heels for too long. A little anticipation was good, but one mustn't overdo it on a first date.

"Honey, you're the most handsome thing." She batted her eyelashes behind those dark glasses. "You put a girl to shame."

"Never that," he smoothly replied. "A mere mortal couldn't outshine a star."

Verrick bit her cheeks to hold back a choking sound. He

was an expert. Without losing a breath, he was giving her mother a dose of her own behavior.

Elly was lapping it up as he held her coat for her and played the adoring male.

And he was playing. Verrick could tell by the way his mustache twitched as he restrained himself from laughing. He stroked the back of Verrick's neck with his fingertips as he helped her on with her own coat, a silent tribute. Like conspirators, they were participating in this performance together.

Dazzling in a sequined plum-colored gown, more glittery than Verrick's tooth fairy costume, Elly monopolized the conversation as the silver Porsche hummed its way to the restaurant. It was as smooth to ride in as it looked from outside. Exactly the thing Elly favored.

At the elaborate restaurant, Lionel checked their coats and guided the ladies toward the maitre d'. Verrick's eyes were agog, the place looked like a French boudoir, flocked red wallpaper, gilt-edged mirrors, heavy velvet draperies and barely enough light to see from the candles and dimly-lit chandeliers.

Elly loved it. "Simply charming," she gushed. Lionel had her by the arm, leading her to their reserved table. With her dark glasses and high heels, she was in danger of falling and breaking an ankle.

"I hope you don't mind . . . but I've invited a few friends to join us."

Verrick squashed the first thought that came to mind. They must be *good* friends to agree to eat in a place like this. She could see through a beaded curtain, blackjack tables and other gambling facilities in the adjoining room. She looked around for a stage, surely there had to be strippers.

This wasn't the usual sort of place Mr. Parford would take a lady.

Even in the dim lighting, he could read her expressive

face. He leaned down and whispered into her ear, "The food is good."

They'd reached their table and his friends stood up to greet them—four dapper gentlemen, each in their sixties, all in black ties and laying on the charm for Elly. Each kissed her hand and helped her to be seated with the most gallant behavior. It was completely overdone. Elly thought it was heaven.

Lionel's plan was cunning—distract Elly with enough eligible men around the table and he wouldn't have to spend the whole evening extricating himself from her clutches.

"Very clever," Verrick whispered as he held out her chair for her.

He kept a straight face, totally innocent, as if he had no idea what she was implying.

She hadn't guessed he concocted this whole scene to get some time alone with her. He seated himself beside her and immediately the wine steward arrived for their orders, then the waiter with menus. This evening was going to cost him a fortune, but drastic measures were required to catch the elusive tooth fairy for an evening.

With liberal amounts of alcohol, Elly and the four older men had a grand time, in a ribald sort of way.

"Did you have to pay them?"

The warmth of his brown eyes showed he didn't take offense. "No . . . I called in a few favors."

"How did you find a place like this?"

"An interior decorator told me about it."

Verrick laughed. Elly was too busy during dinner to pay Lionel Parford any attention. "I could never have thought up such a devious plan. You're amazing."

"I do my best to please."

They were in the midst of a raucous party but it seemed like an intimate dinner for two. The food was well-prepared and the single glass of white wine they each had was excellent. No one noticed their quiet conversation or lack of participation in the party atmosphere at their table.

"Has your mother been in an accident . . . or has she had surgery on her eyes?"

"My mother? Did she tell you?"

"No, not Elly."

"Then how did you know?"

"Your legs."

"My legs?"

He nodded and swallowed her with such a devouring look, she blushed. Although she thought no one could see in the flickering shadows cast by the candles, Lionel Parford saw it.

"Great legs aren't all that common. It's unlikely two women would have the same sensational legs and not be related. The age difference is too great for sisters. You must be mother and daughter. Am I wrong?"

"No. Elly is my mother. And no, she wasn't in an accident. She had cosmetic surgery." She leaned closer and confided, "Under those dark glasses she looks like a raccoon."

He placed his large hand over hers where it rested on the table—a warm, comforting gesture. "Doesn't want her friends to see it?"

"Something like that. Her home's in Calgary. She's going to stay with me until the bruising fades."

He stroked her hand. "You're a good daughter."

That choked her up. She hoped he couldn't see tears brimming in her eyes. She hadn't been a daughter at all; nor had Elly been a mother. She grew up in day care and boarding school. She never had a permanent home, a room to call her own, a bicycle, or anything resembling a family. What would he know about such things with that delightful mother of his, married only once and living in the same house all those years?

It pained him to see the sadness in her beautiful eyes.

He squeezed her hand. "Perhaps the future holds what the past did not."

That sparked such hope, she looked at him, grateful for his understanding. He really was very handsome when he looked at her like that.

"Yes, Jenna. He took us out to dinner."

"Both you and Elly?"

"And four men picked to overwhelm my mother."

"Far out! Who'd have thought it?"

"Mr. Parford thought of it. And it's kept my mother occupied, she's talked of nothing else for three whole days."

"How is the old girl?"

"She's recovering from plastic surgery to remove the bags under her eyes. Are you free to join us for dinner tonight?"

"I'd love to. Elly's always good for a laugh. Are you inviting your neighbor, too?"

"No. Spare him. He's done more than enough already."

He would like to do more but Verrick Grant was a hard woman to get near. It was November, the daylight hours were getting shorter, and he hadn't encountered her on the beach again, even though he faithfully jogged the route on which he met her. She didn't loiter in the hallway, and if she used the swimming pool, he hadn't figured out when. Her car was gone all day, she worked regular hours. Funny, her job didn't come up in their conversations. He still didn't know what she did for a living.

"Lion, is something bothering you?"

"No, Mother. Just building castles in the air."

"How like an architect. Do you have some new project you're working on?"

"I've been commissioned to design a private home for a Hong Kong family. They have some very specific requirements. They are happy with the blueprints I've showed them, but it got me to thinking about the sort of family home I would like for myself."

Sonya Parford listened attentively, giving no indication of her surprise. This was the first mention Lionel ever made about having a family or building himself a home. Was there a woman involved in these plans? Her serene face betrayed none of her curiosity as she absorbed her son's words.

"I saw a lovely piece of property near Langley, several acres, south facing, nicely treed, perfect for a family home. I've made an offer on the land, if it goes through, and there's no reason it shouldn't, I'll be ready to start building within the month."

"That sounds most exciting, dear. There's nothing more challenging than getting one's own home exactly right. We've been in this house forty years, and there are still a few things that need adjusting."

"It may be a challenge but it's one I'm looking forward to."

Birgit came in with a tea tray and any further chance to question Lionel about his plans passed.

As he sipped his hot tea, Sonya noticed him wince, as though in pain. "Is a tooth bothering you, dear?"

"One of my molars . . . just a little sensitive. It will pass."

"Don't let it go on too long. Nothing is worse than a toothache. I know how you hate dentists, but promise you'll call one if that pain persists."

"I'll have it looked at, Mother. I promise. It's probably nothing."

"Jenna, honey, aren't you married yet?"

"No, Elly. You know how it is—all the attractive men are either happily married, gay, or about to enter the priesthood."

"That's nonsense. You have to get out there and shop."

Jenna and Verrick shared a knowing glance. Shopping was Elly's favorite pastime.

"Finding the right man is like shopping for shoes."

Verrick giggled but Jenna kept a straight face. "How's that, Elly?"

"Sometimes you see a gorgeous pair you must have, but when you try them on, they pinch with every step."

"Husband number one," Verrick whispered to her friend.

"If you buy them, you get blisters and they make you miserable. You stick them in the closet and never wear them again."

"I've had that happen," Jenna admitted, but with shoes not with husbands.

"But don't give up," Elly continued. "Sometimes you see a dull pair but they fit perfectly."

"Husband number two," Verrick whispered.

"Then you decide if you're willing to settle for less than perfect. Is being comfortable enough? Can you live with a homely pair or do you need a little glamor?"

"It sounds like you're speaking from experience, Mother."

"Honey lamb, you have to try on a lot of shoes before you find the perfect pair."

"How do you recognize the perfect pair?"

"You absolutely must have them, and when you slip them on, they feel made especially for your feet. That's the perfect pair."

"What if you don't enjoy shopping?"

"Then you're stuck, aren't you? You have to make do, settle for less than the best until something better comes along."

"Husband number three?" Jenna asked. Verrick nodded.

"Well," Verrick stated. "I'm happy to go barefoot."

"Honey child, you can't mean that. A nice pair of shoes feels good and is flattering, if you choose well."

"What if I can't afford them?"

"You have to pay the price. Good shoes don't come cheap."

"I'm not willing to do without important things to afford the shoes of my dreams."

"I don't know how a daughter of mine can be so cold-hearted."

"Mother, you have to admit, your favorite pair of shoes, no matter how expensive, eventually wears out."

Jenna held up four fingers and Verrick nodded.

"True . . . you can't wear a pair scruffy and out of shape . . . but that frees you to start shopping again."

Jenna and Verrick snickered through clearing the table and washing the dinner dishes. Elly was one of a kind.

"Well, girl," Verrick mimicked. "You and I have got to get out there shopping for shoes." They burst into giggles.

Only Elly would come up with such an idea.

Chapter Five

"We're going to Whistler this weekend to open the house for the ski season. Will you join us, Lion?"

"Little early for skiing isn't it?"

"The snow pack isn't deep, but there's good skiing on the glaciers. And the party scene is in full swing."

"The party scene is always swinging at Whistler."

"You're showing your age, big brother. That retirement haven you live in is making you old before your time."

Gavin heard his brother's low growl, clear across town, on the other end of the telephone. Lionel was fun to tease; he acted the austere, gruff, stuffed shirt so well, but his brother wasn't fooled. There was a heart beating behind that stern exterior. As the oldest child, he felt a responsibility to look after the younger ones and Gavin didn't think he allowed himself to have fun often enough.

"Laureen Geddis is hinting she'd like to spend the weekend at our chalet. Are you planning on inviting her?"

"No." One single word was all he uttered. He and Laureen were often seen as a couple, but this morning she had completely lost her appeal. Strangely, her charms suddenly seemed grating, her voice too shrill, her perfume too overpowering, her clothes too flashy. Maybe Gavin was right, he was getting old.

"Shucks! I was hoping you'd invite Laureen." Lionel couldn't see it, but Gavin was grinning ear to ear. "That would clear the way for me to invite the tooth fairy."

Lionel disappointed his brother and didn't respond.

"I'd like to check the heating system in the chalet. Perhaps I will come this weekend."

Holding back laughter, Gavin had a hard time keeping his voice from cracking. "Great. We'll see you Saturday, then."

He put the telephone down, and the laughter burbled up to join that of his twin sister.

"Gavin, that was wicked. Do you think he'll ask her?"

The idea had been planted and it germinated in the back of his mind for the rest of the day. Finally, he took action.

Lionel towered over his secretary's desk. "Mrs. Ross, find me the telephone number for a Miss Verrick Grant. It should be a new listing." He strode back to his drafting table to finish the sketch of the home so much in his mind lately.

Gavin wasn't going to get an unchallenged path to the tooth fairy if he had anything to say about it.

"I'm sorry, sir. That number is unlisted."

"All right, Mrs. Ross. I'll have to deal with it in person."

His secretary scurried back to her desk. Mr. Parford didn't look at all pleased.

Later that evening, the silver Porsche pulled in beside an empty parking space. She wasn't home. Impatiently he locked his car and stalked up the four flights of stairs with a scowl on his face.

He thrust his briefcase onto a chair and changed into his jogging clothes. It was a gray November day with a chilly breeze off the water but Lionel Parford ran the length of the promenade and back before he felt his customary calm spirits return.

He didn't know what had gotten into him; he wasn't usually so irritable over nothing.

He was sweaty, his hair damp and disheveled, and his shirt moist and clinging in spots. But Verrick didn't see him. She was busy preparing dinner and had no idea her immaculate neighbor could look as grubby and unkempt as any ordinary mortal.

When he knocked on her door later that evening, he had showered and shaved and was wearing a black turtleneck sweater over hip-hugging jeans. No traces of the sweaty jogger remained.

"Hello. My mother left for Calgary this afternoon, if you came to see her." Verrick couldn't imagine Mr. Parford would seek out her company. She had little conceit and no idea of her appeal.

"No . . . it was you I wanted to see."

"Come in then." She was surprised but didn't let it show. Instead, she chattered on, "I'm drinking apple juice, will you join me or would you like something stronger?"

"Apple juice will be fine." He followed her into her living room, softly lit with table lamps. He'd designed this building, and his own apartment had a similar floor plan, but she'd made hers distinctive, quite different from his. He liked it. It invited a person to sit down and be comfortable. Which is just what he did.

Verrick handed him a mug. The apple juice was heated and she placed a dish of graham wafers on the low table in front of him. As nimbly as a cat, she folded herself into a sitting position on the carpet and smiled up at him. She wasn't going to be kept in suspense a minute longer.

"What did you want to see me about?"

He detected the note of apprehension in her voice. "Couldn't it be a neighborly visit?"

"Not likely."

That surprised him and it showed on his startled face, his eyebrows rose questioningly, he lowered his chin and looked down into her upturned face. His voice was quiet when he spoke.

"Oh. Why's that?"

"We aren't exactly best buddies. You give me disapproving looks whenever our paths cross and sometimes you wiggle your nose as if you've smelled something nasty when we meet."

"I don't wiggle my nose."

"Yes you do. And you inhale as if you're trying to get a breath of fresh air."

On that point he was guilty as charged. No other woman he'd met smelled like a profusion of lilacs in spring. "Then I apologize. It wasn't intentional."

"Oh, I knew that. You're too polite to let on that I offend you." She smiled at him with gentle understanding.

This wasn't going as he planned. He'd intended to invite her for a weekend at his family's chalet, not be informed he was a snob and found her offensive. He was reeling from her accusations. This was a new experience. She made no attempt to flirt or attract attention to herself. He was bewildered. He looked so downcast, Verrick tried to soften the blow.

"But you were very nice inviting my mother for dinner. I never had a chance to properly thank you so I'll do it now. I really appreciated what you did. The restaurant could have been from a B grade movie, but your gesture had class. It was creative, the mark of a true gentleman. Thank you."

Verrick looked him straight in his confounded brown eyes and meant every word she said. It was unlike any thank you he'd ever received before.

Perhaps now was a good time to extend his invitation. Before she had a chance to scramble his wits further.

He straightened his shoulders, trying to gather his shattered dignity. She looked like an innocent child sitting on the floor looking up at him. But she was a grown woman who had just thanked him and insulted him, if he remembered correctly.

"The reason for my visit . . . was to invite you to my family's winter chalet at Whistler for the weekend. I believe you've already met my brother, Gavin . . . he'll be there and several other family members as well."

"Did you design the chalet?"

"Yes, as a matter of fact, I did."

"Is it all logs and glass and big stone fireplaces?"

"Yes, that describes it quite well." He was losing his train of thought. She had the ability to totally confuse him. He put his invitation into words, before she muddled him further. "As I started to say . . . we're going to check the chalet and be sure it's stocked and ready for the ski season. I came to ask if you'd like to accompany me for the day, or we could stay the weekend, there's plenty of room."

It may have come out a little disjointed but it was said. He relaxed into his armchair and waited for her answer.

She didn't think it over more than a few seconds before she responded. "Thank you for the invitation. But no. I'm not into the ski scene."

Mr. Perfect was dumbfounded. She didn't soften the blow, say she had previous plans or leave it open for another time. She said flat out NO.

She didn't look angry or spiteful, on the contrary, she looked delightful, munching graham wafers and studying him with her soulful blue eyes. Should he ask for further explanation? Or did he take no for what it was—a definite refusal? He chose the latter.

Verrick took pity on him.

"It isn't you . . . it's the ski scene I don't like."

If that was an olive branch, it didn't help much. "Would you like to elaborate?"

"My father was a world class skier . . ."

"Your father is Reggie Grant?"

"That's right. When it was his turn to have me for school vacations, they were always at trendy ski slopes with the latest in a chain of ski bunnies." The painful note in her voice was more revealing than her words. "So, I don't have pleasant associations with the ski scene. I'm sorry, but I don't want to go to Whistler."

"Where is your father now?"

"He's in Florida, with his third wife and new baby daughter."

"He doesn't ski anymore?"

"His latest wife is smart, she doesn't want to compete with ski bunnies. There isn't any skiing in Florida."

"Thanks for explaining. For a while there, I thought I'd lost my charm."

"You have nothing to worry about. You have charm by the bucket load." She gave him an impish grin. "I won't tell anyone if you don't."

"Then my reputation is safe."

They were both able to laugh at that remark. He was still off balance.

Verrick Grant was a new experience. No other woman had refused a weekend at Whistler. She wasn't impressed by wealth or trendy ski resorts.

He returned to his apartment bewildered but determined. Somehow, he'd find what did impress Verrick Grant.

The weekend at Whistler was a success. He avoided Laureen Geddis, he fine-tuned the heating system, checked the chalet for wear and tear, and enjoyed an invigorating afternoon hike with members of his family.

"So, did you invite the tooth fairy?"

"She turned me down."

"Poor Lion. I could knock out one of your teeth. Maybe she'd come then."

"Very funny. Even that wouldn't do it."

Rachel was interested in this conversation. "Why, Lion? What did you do to the woman?" She gave her scolding frown and shook her finger in front of his nose. "Have you been acting king of the beasts with her?"

"It seems I have."

His relatives gathered around the fireplace, their curiosity roused.

"Why do you say that?"

"She said I wiggle my nose as if I've smelled something nasty."

Rachel hooted. "She noticed! She must be clever. How are you going to win her over, Lion?"

"No one said anything about winning her over."

He didn't say anything about winning her over, but he couldn't hide the fact he was interested. Gavin and Rachel knew their older brother well. He may look cool and unruffled on the surface but underneath he was definitely interested.

Verrick Grant was an intriguing woman. He'd find a way to spend more time with her.

He did. But it wasn't what he'd planned.

Jenna arrived with a loaded truck and a crew from props and costumes to set up the starlight ballroom for the movie shoot.

"What are all these things?" Verrick examined a rusty tray of ancient surgical equipment. "Handcuffs? Dog collars? And what's this—a bowl of fake ice cubes? The place looks like a torture chamber not a doctor's home."

"Remember, girl, a doctor with a dark side, kinky, in other words."

"Where do you want this couch, Jenna?"

Two men carried in an unusual black leather piece of furniture with sharp metal studs outlining one side.

"Put it here," Jenna gestured. "Under the skylight. Perfect."

Verrick cringed and shook her head. The addition of bandages, surgical gauze and knives of every shape and size on a stainless steel table made the starlight ballroom look downright creepy.

She hadn't seen anything yet. The chains and headless dressmaker's dummy added a surreal touch, along with the whips and the white lab coat. She was glad this was pretend; she'd hate to meet a doctor with a home like this in real life.

"I saw your neighbor in the lobby. How's it going between you two?"

"Cool and distant."

"I thought he took you and Elly out for dinner."

"That was for Elly's benefit."

"What's the problem?"

"He scares me, Jenna. If he only had one glaring flaw I could feel more comfortable with him. I can't believe he's for real."

"Could be worse. He could be obnoxious."

"That I could deal with. No one's attracted to obnoxious."

"Aha! Then you admit you're attracted?"

"Okay. I admit I'm attracted . . . but scared, too."

"Scared of what?"

"Losing my sanity. Men who seem so perfect and handsome only exist in movies and novels; in real life those kind of men can't be trusted, Jenna. Look at my mother's track record—heart breakers, every one."

"Elly isn't suffering."

"But I'm not Elly. A broken heart would kill me. I'm terrified to risk it."

"Cheer up, honey lamb. It's as easy as shopping for shoes."

"Don't remind me, I'm still recovering from my mother's visit."

Jenna couldn't say anything to convince Verrick that taking the risk was worth it. Mr. Parford was going to have to do that on his own. She quickly changed the subject.

"The shoot is scheduled for tomorrow. You okay with that?"

"Fine. I hope I can sleep with that stuff in the starlight ballroom tonight. It makes me feel a sadistic ghoul is on the loose."

"Then we've done a good job. See you tomorrow."

"Verrick, I have a patient I'd like to refer to you. He has a terror of dentists and even annual check-ups have become increasingly difficult."

"Does he come to the office willingly?"

"Yes. He wants to overcome his fear but it's a losing battle. It's an instinctive reaction he's not proud of."

"What caused the fear?"

"Some childhood accident, broken front tooth, dental work without freezing. The kid went through so much pain he's been traumatized ever since."

"Does he require hospitalization and full sedation?"

"That's the next step. I'd like you to try first. If anyone can help him overcome his panic, you can."

"Have you done an initial examination?"

"Yes. I've taken X-rays. I'll send over his medical charts. He needs a filling on the second lower left molar."

"Does he have a history of heart or breathing problems?"

"No. He's as healthy as an ox except for this one weakness. I've had no success. He's a dentist's worst nightmare."

"How does he react?"

"The instant he steps into the office, all color drains from his face. He sits in the chair, his body goes tense, his pulse accelerates, and his breathing becomes shallow. I've tried to talk him through it but I can see his eyes frantically darting from my face to my assistant to the tools in my hand."

"Has he fainted?"

"Not yet, but his blood pressure shoots way up."

"Sounds extreme."

"Believe me, it is. You're his last hope. Will you accept the case?"

"I'll do my best."

"Good. I'll send over his dental records, medical charts and X-rays. I've done a thorough examination. I'll send you those findings, as well."

"Have you prescribed sedatives for him to take before office visits?"

"He refuses them."

"Is he in pain at the moment?"

"Yes. The tooth is sensitive to heat and cold. I'd say it's bothering him a lot."

"Okay. I'll schedule him right away."

After hanging up the phone, she realized she hadn't asked the child's age. "Poor kid, he's probably throbbing with pain and shaking with fear at this very moment."

The reception area was pleasant, no white coats or face masks, no indication of this being a medical office, except walls of files behind the area where eight pleasant women were seated with telephones and computers, dressed in street clothes, and welcoming him with cheerful smiles. A waiting area was furnished with comfortable chairs, tall potted plants, a play space with bright toys for children, all in soothing subdued colors.

He didn't get to sit in one of those chairs in the waiting room. As soon as he held out his appointment card to one of the smiling women, she handed it to the appropriate receptionist and he was greeted by name and an attractive young woman appeared to escort him to the office. For a moment, he thought she was going to take his hand or pat him on the head.

Instead, she smiled and said, "How nice to have you visit. We've been expecting you."

She didn't mention that Dr. Grant had fully prepared her for their two o'clock appointment—a panic case—referred by Dr. Corman. At first, she expected a frightened child, but the dental records showed adult teeth, and this tall virile specimen she was leading to the dentist's chair was definitely not a child. If she weren't a married woman she'd be drooling—he was that gorgeous.

The dental assistant was about to show their two o'clock patient into the soothing, adult-oriented Room One, but Dr. Grant forestalled her and motioned to Room Two, the children's trauma room. It was a delight in soft colors, animals on the wallpaper, a ceiling mural painted with sky, sun, and cheery faces and little surprises peeking out from behind puffy clouds. There were stuffed toys and a hat rack with weird and wonderful costumes—a cowboy hat, feathered headdresses, pirate's hat, fire chief's red hat, plus capes, aprons and scarves for dress up.

Nothing in the room looked like a dentist's office, even the examining chair was of soft blue fabric and looked inviting rather than threatening.

Karen was well trained. She seated the patient in the chair immediately, all the dental tools and equipment situated behind his line of vision.

Neither the ingenious design nor the modern efficiency registered on the patient, now seated in the dentist's chair. He was mesmerized by the woman wearing a frilled pink apron and a tiara, perched on a stool beside his chair.

To say he was surprised would be an understatement. He was shocked, something Verrick considered an advantage. All the less likely his panic would set in right away.

"You're a dentist?!"

Her blue eyes sparkled from behind large glasses, and she answered in the sweet tooth fairy voice he'd heard before. "Lionel, I make-believe a lot of things, but I'm a real-life qualified dentist."

He was so startled, he hadn't noticed Karen attach a bib around his neck, adjust his chair, or position the lights.

Verrick held his attention and kept chattering. "We have something special for you today, not strawberry or mint or anything boring like that." She dampened a cotton swab and passed it beneath his nose—piña colada. "Smell that. Doesn't that smell wonderful? And wait till you taste it."

She slipped the swab inside his mouth and stroked the gum beneath the painful tooth. She and Karen had studied his charts and Dr. Corman's notes and knew exactly where to zero in.

Karen nodded and Verrick kept up her patter.

"Can't you just taste the coconut in that?" He had to admit it did taste like piña colada but he didn't get time to savor it, the outrageous woman was staring down at him wide-eyed.

She looked over his whole reclining length and dropped her voice to a seductive purr. "My, you're a big boy." His mouth gaped opened in shock as she gestured to his feet reaching to the end of the chair. He didn't feel the needle entering his gum, numbed by the cotton swab, he was too busy glowering at the woman's tiara, thinking there must be laws protecting patients from sexual harassment.

Verrick winked at Karen.

They needed to give the freezing time to take. If anyone could, Dr. Grant would keep his mind off the fact he was in a dentist's chair. She was getting more outrageous by the second. It was too good a performance not to share. Karen flicked open the intercom to the outer office.

"Now, Lionel, that mustache will have to go. I can't see into your mouth with those bristle brush tufts of hair covering your lip."

He glared at her, the fury in his eyes threatening agony for Verrick if she dared to shave off his mustache. But she didn't give him a chance to speak. She could imagine the curses that would escape his lips if she let him open his mouth at this moment.

"Whatever do men see in having hair under their nose? Madness, I say." Dr. Grant had told Karen to closely monitor this patient's breathing and pulse. He looked ready to explode but when she gently put her fingers around his wrist, his pulse was steady and normal.

Verrick received the nod.

He was about to open his mouth to respond but she

raised her hands in mock horror. "Where are my manners? Lionel, I haven't introduced you to Karen." Her assistant smiled and shook his hand.

"Karen is my firefighter." On cue, she reached up and put on the bright red fire chief's hat. "You know it's hard for women to get hired fighting fires, so we have to humor Karen. Otherwise, she gets upset. Life can be so unfair."

Lionel Parford was about to choke, but Verrick kept his lovely brown eyes focussed directly on her.

"Karen has a tiny little hose for spraying water and another little hose that sucks it back up. Let's practice, Lionel." She bent over and whispered in his ear, "She's very good."

That sounded so suggestive, and with him laid out in such a vulnerable position, his jaw dropped.

Karen seized the moment. She sprayed the tooth in question, then suctioned the area dry. The patient showed no reaction, made no movement, felt no pain. The freezing had taken. She gave Dr. Grant the all clear signal.

"Before I take a look in your mouth, Lionel, you'll have to promise to do something for me."

She pressed a large stuffed bear into his grasp. "This is Mr. Cuddles. He's had a dreadful experience. Mr. Cuddles loves honey and when he followed his nose to the sweetest honey he'd ever smelled, a swarm of bees came after him and he got stung six times.

"Now he doesn't like buzzing sounds. They make him think of bee stings. So whenever you hear a buzzing sound, you must hug him very tight. Do you think you can do that for me?"

His look of disbelief gave some hint of what he'd like to do to her.

She kept asking him ridiculous questions but never gave him a chance to answer. She kept him completely off balance.

"Let's practice that, shall we? I'm going to take a look

in your mouth and if you hear bees buzzing near, hug Mr. Cuddles as tight as you can."

"Now, open wide."

He opened without objection. She began drilling the cavity that had been giving him so much pain.

She pulled back and gave her patient a scolding look. "Now, Lionel, that wasn't very good at all. When you hear the buzzing noise, you must hug Mr. Cuddles tightly. Let him know he's safe. Being stung by bees is a serious matter."

She closed his fingers around the furry stuffed bear. "We're going to try that again. This time I want you to try harder."

Giving Karen the signal, she completed the drilling as her assistant kept the mouth clear with suction, no saliva or bits of drilled enamel were left to irritate the unsuspecting patient. His hands were clenched around the bear's neck in a demonstration of how he wished to strangle Dr. Grant.

Verrick patted his shoulder. "Good boy. That was much better."

Sparks were flying from his eyes. She couldn't tell if they were from anger, shock, horror, or indignity. But she did know they were not from pain, and that was all she was concerned with at the moment.

Karen received the silent instruction to prepare the filling compound.

The sugary sweet voice of the tooth fairy was gone and Verrick's own gentle lilting voice replaced it.

"Do you brush carefully and floss regularly?"

He was being treated as a naughty boy and taking it like a good sport but she talked so much he couldn't get his wits together long enough to form a reply.

"Open up and let me see."

The silly woman hadn't even asked which tooth was bothering him, yet. He opened his mouth, surprised to be feeling no pain. Lately, the slightest intake of breath across the offending tooth made him wince in agony.

Verrick inserted the filling compound into the cavity, pressed it down and shaped it.

"Oh dear, Lionel. I see some spots where you haven't been flossing carefully."

That was the least of his worries. Throbbing pain was the reason he was in this chair, not to have some lecture on cleaning his teeth.

The thunder in his eyes gave her warning. So she upped the level of distraction.

"Thorough flossing is as important as safe sky diving. You must never be careless."

Tears trickled from the corners of Karen's eyes as she choked back laughter.

Lionel Parford's wide eyes were harder to interpret.

"Don't look so shocked, dear boy. Even fairies,"—there was a dramatic pause—"especially fairies . . . know about sky diving."

The receptionists in the outer office were passing a box of Kleenex, trying to maintain decorum fitting a dentist office but they huddled near the open intercom, straining to overhear the scene being acted out in Dr. Grant's office.

The receptionist's voice wobbled dangerously as she chimed Dr. Grant's room. "Your next appointment has arrived, Linda Barlow and her mother."

"Thank you, Mary. Send Linda down but give Mrs. Barlow a cup of coffee and keep her in the waiting room."

Karen disappeared to bring Linda to Dr. Grant's examining room.

Lionel Parford moved his lips and finally was given the chance to speak. "Well, get on with it! Your next patient has arrived and you haven't even begun on me."

The tooth fairy's voice was back. "Oh, but I have, Mr. Parford. I've been working you over since the instant you came in."

"You can say that again."

Verrick raised the dentist chair to a sitting position.

"Avoid hot or cold and keep from biting down on that for the next hour."

He remained sitting in the chair, stunned, his hand to his cheek.

"All finished, Mr. Parford. Next time, don't let the cavity get so advanced before you come to see me."

He ran his tongue over his filled tooth.

"And for being such a brave boy, I have a special badge for you. She pinned it on the lapel of his immaculate charcoal gray suit. It said, "I saw the tooth fairy."

"Karen will show you the way to the waiting room." She bent and whispered in his ear, "That's where it really hurts. They give you your bill."

She glided into another examining room and he could hear her cheerful voice begin chatting with a little girl.

A dentist's waiting room was not Lionel Parford's idea of a cheerful place to work, yet all of the women were smiling and seemed very happy. They made eye contact, warm and friendly as if they knew him well, even though this was his first visit. He didn't expect the handmaidens of the torturers to be so gleeful about it.

The office staff waited for the waiting room door to close and then listened for the sound of the elevator starting down.

Then the receptionists and office staff for all eight dentists practicing out of the office slumped over their keyboards and howled with laughter.

Waiting dental patients, not knowing the cause, were caught up in the mirth, grinning and chuckling because it was so contagious. For several minutes, no one spoke, tissues were passed around, eyes dried, and office-like faces composed.

The first dental assistant to regain her voice gasped in nawe, "That deserves an Academy Award." Then the giggles started again.

"Did you see the 'I saw the tooth fairy' badge on his suit?"

"It went with his lopsided smile. His left side was half frozen."

"I knew Dr. Grant was good with trauma patients, but he didn't even know she'd filled his tooth."

"It's a miracle he didn't have a heart attack, some of the things she said."

Thankfully, it was near the end of doctor's hours. The staff in the outer office never fully recovered their composure that day.

The man in the descending elevator saw his one-sided smile reflected from the glass above the control panel. If he hadn't been alone in the elevator, people would have wondered what was so funny.

The tall, dignified man in the somber business suit laughed out loud and shook his head in disbelief.

Swiping his hand across his eyes, he unlocked his car door and slid behind the steering wheel.

"That woman is priceless!"

Chapter Six

The lights were positioned, the sound equipment set up, and cameras waiting. The only thing missing was darkness outside the starlight ballroom, casting its eerie shadows, concealing and revealing the distorted private life of the mysterious doctor. Cast and crew had adjourned until after sunset to film the scene in the murky light of night-time hours. Only Jenna remained when Verrick returned home.

"How did the shoot go this morning?"

"Super. It's a very short sequence, only two actors involved, but the starlight ballroom speaks volumes. We're going to try it again this evening when the light fades. The director thinks it will add that extra touch of weirdness."

Verrick thought it looked quite weird enough in broad daylight.

"Jenna, girl, I worry about you." She swept her hand to encompass the starlight ballroom. "If you can think up a set like this, what else lurks in that mind of yours?"

Imitating an old radio show, Jenna answered in a spooky voice, "Only the Shadow knows."

They shared the joy of acting, movies and film, and the escape it provided. And they both were aware of the danger in avoiding real life problems by hiding behind make-believe. It took a strong person to deal with every day realities and never escape into role playing. Only with close friends could these two women be vulnerable, only then could the masks come off and the real personality shine through.

Together they began dinner preparations, Jenna peeling vegetables while Verrick tossed a salad.

"How was today in the life of a dentist?"

"I had an interesting patient."

"Do tell."

"Mr. Parford was referred to me by Dr. Corman."

"And . . . ?"

"And . . . I discovered a dent in his shining armor."

"Well, girl, now's your chance. Shout it from the roof-tops. Bring the man to his knees."

Verrick's compassionate nature was mirrored in her serious face. "It wouldn't be professional. You see, his weakness is . . . he hates dentists."

Jenna let out a whoop of disbelief. "You mean the stuffed shirt who excels at everything, with every hair in place, and no visible flaws, falls to pieces at the word 'dentist'?"

Verrick nodded. "That's his weakness."

"Tell me more."

"There's not much to tell. I filled his tooth . . ."

"And . . . ?"

"And he went away."

"Verrick. You're leaving something out. You filled his tooth? Just as easy as that?"

"Well . . . I had to distract him."

"What did you do?"

"I threatened to shave off his mustache." Verrick paused to think about the two o'clock appointment in her office. "And I gave him a teddy bear to hold."

Jenna laughed outright. "How did he take it?"

"He was too stunned to react."

"He won't be for long. Watch out, girl, when the freezing wears off, reaction will set in. He'll want revenge."

"Oh, I don't think so. I think he was glad to get out of the office alive. I'm sure he never wants to set eyes on me again."

Jenna didn't believe that for a minute, not the way Lionel Parford looked at Verrick. "He'll recover."

"I'm not so sure. Terror of dentists goes deep. I think he'll avoid me like the plague from now on."

"That's going to be hard. He lives next door."

Verrick considered this for a moment. She may have filled his tooth but it was highly unlikely she'd done anything to lessen his fear and loathing of dentists. "He'll find a way to banish me from his life. There's nothing he can't do. Remember, he's Mr. Perfect."

The freezing had worn off and reaction did set in. Lionel Parford was astounded at the ease with which Dr. Grant had filled his tooth without his usual panic attack rearing its ugly head.

Since childhood, he'd dreaded the dentist after having a tooth broken while at hockey camp and having a dentist work on it without the benefit of freezing. The pain had been enough to make him black out. Ever since, he was terrified of a dentist's chair, unreasonable as it was and as hard as he tried to overcome it. Overpowering fear from somewhere deep inside took over the instant he set foot in a dentist's office. Considering that, Dr. Grant had performed a miracle.

He marvelled how good he was feeling. He was not trembling or nauseous and didn't have a headache or upset stomach. In fact, he enjoyed a full dinner, no throbbing pain in his jaw, no tenderness when he chewed. And even more remarkable, if he remembered correctly, he had actually felt like laughing as he left the dentist office.

The amazing woman set his mind spinning, he never had a chance to realize what she was up to. He tentatively bit down on the tooth that had been so painful these past weeks. Nothing. He bit down harder. Not a glimmer of tenderness. This was the first meal he'd been able to eat comfortably in days.

Much could be said about Verrick Grant, but one thing was certain—she was an excellent dentist.

He would like to express his appreciation. In his wildest imaginings, he never thought he could enjoy a dentist visit. She had accomplished the impossible.

It took a little getting used to, the idea his neighbor was a dentist. It made sense if he put all the little bits he'd noticed about her together. The clothes she wore to work each morning first caught his attention. He'd guessed she might be a hairdresser.

Then there were her hands, she had lovely hands—well-kept, neatly trimmed nails, none of those long claws painted in bright colors. A dentist worked with her hands. But he never suspected.

He did wonder how she could afford to live in Westerly Place. It was an expensive building to buy into. But when he tried to investigate, he'd only been able to find out that she'd paid for her condominium in full. From the outrageous look of some of her visitors and the glassy unfocused stare she aimed his way, he briefly suspected she dealt drugs. That would explain her money.

But Westerly Place had demanded character references and Verrick Grant's were stellar. Doctors, if he recalled correctly, all sang her praises.

There was nothing about her appearance or her behavior that would have made him guess her profession. Never in a thousand years. He didn't think of dentists as human, and definitely not attractive. She had him fooled.

She didn't sign her name as Dr. Grant, she never gave any clue about the work she did.

Well, being the tooth fairy could have been a hint. She did it so convincingly.

Did knowing what she did for a living change anything?

He was her patient, did that eliminate any chance of forming a personal relationship?

He'd never imagined wanting to form a personal relationship with a dentist. Until today, they had been the enemy, bringers of pain and morbid torturers. That didn't describe Verrick Grant.

He placed the dinner dishes in his dishwasher, still struggling with the fact that she was a dentist—the most feared and hated of professions.

Darkness added that extra spooky quality the director wanted. The scene was shot quickly, having been gone through already earlier in the day. Cameras, lighting, sound equipment were all packed and wheeled out to the elevator and into a waiting truck. Jenna would remove the props and costumes later in the week. It had been a successful filming and everyone left in good spirits.

Lionel Parford's eyes widened in surprise as he observed the man leaving Verrick Grant's door. He was wearing black leather pants but naked from the waist up, a heavy muscular man, his head shaved and glistening in the hall light. Several serpent-like tattoos twined up his arms and a vicious snake head in blue and red was tattooed across his chest. There was a silver ring through his ear and another through his lip. He was not the sort of man Lionel would want to meet in a deserted alley in the dark of night. What in the world was he doing coming out of his neighbor's suite?

The half-naked man saw censure in the eyes of the conservatively dressed man coming toward him down the hall. He leered at him, showing sharpened front teeth. "Evening," he growled low in his throat as he passed, heading for the elevator.

This was a day of firsts for Lionel Parford. He'd never met a character like that—he thought they only existed in gangster movies.

Still off balance, he knocked on Verrick's door. She opened it, visibly surprised to see her neighbor. A look of concern clouded her clear blue eyes. "Mr. Parford . . . are you in pain?"

"No. Not at all. I merely wanted to . . ." At this point Jenna came to see who was at the door, thinking perhaps one of her crew had forgotten something.

Verrick stood back and invited her neighbor to enter. "Lionel Parford, this is my friend, Jenna Wilson." They shook hands and moved down the hall to the living room.

"Jenna and I were just having a cup of tea. Will you join us?"

"Thank you." He remembered those were the words he'd come to say, but with her friend here, it seemed inappropriate to express his appreciation for what she'd done this afternoon. He looked bewildered and Verrick took pity on him.

"Has your tooth been bothering you?"

"No. It's fine. I . . ." He paused, staring over Verrick's shoulder into the starlight ballroom. The light was faint but he couldn't miss the stainless steel table and rusty surgical tools on the metal-studded leather bench. He held his teacup halfway to his mouth and stared. A familiar knot of fear curled up from the pit of his stomach. It was how he'd always imagined a dentist's home to be in his worst nightmares. He blinked and stared again. He wasn't dreaming. He'd walked into the den of the torturer.

Verrick had no idea why Lionel Parford was so tonguetied. But Jenna was holding back a grin by clenching her teeth tightly shut. She could see the direction of his awestruck gaze but she was on the verge of laughter, unable to say anything. The look on his face was worth a million dollars. He was just made for playing pranks on.

He quickly placed his tea cup on the table and stood to leave, mumbling something about not wanting to intrude, then disappeared quickly down the hall, safely behind his own locked door.

Jenna was roaring with laughter but Verrick stood in the middle of the living room brushing the hair out of her eyes with one hand and gesturing toward the door with the other.

"What was that all about?"

Jenna pointed behind Verrick into the starlight ballroom. Then reality dawned.

"Good Lord! He thought all that stuff is for real! Jenna, stop laughing. This is serious. The man rushed out of here thinking I'm a sadistic ghoul."

Jenna nodded her head vigorously, grinning, remembering the horrified look on the man's face.

"I'm doomed," Verrick groaned. "He thinks I'm the kinky doctor you set this up for." She looked into the starlight ballroom trying to see it for the first time as her unsuspecting neighbor had just done. It was gruesome.

"I'll never live this down. I'll be forever labelled as the spooky doctor of Westerly Place." She wanted to be angry with her friend, but she couldn't. It was just too bizarre. Verrick slumped down into the sofa, head in hands, and groaned.

"Poor man, he'll probably never sit in a dentist's chair for as long as he lives. And he'll never cross my path again."

Only a few yellow leaves clung to the bare branches of the alders as Lionel Parford paced the length and breadth of his newly acquired property. It was a beautiful acreage, several tall maples, some wild cherry trees, a few cedars, even a creek running through. It was the ideal spot for a home, on the high ground facing south. He could see it in his mind, kitchen facing east, living room to the west catching the evening light.

He inhaled deeply, crisp November air, then exhaled, his breath forming a steamy cloud. He felt wonderful. Only last week that breath of cold air would have had him writhing in pain. He ran his tongue over his filled tooth. That woman is a miracle worker.

Lionel regretted his hasty retreat the other evening. He never did make clear his genuine appreciation for what she had done. Ever since, the woman had become invisible, scurrying in and out of Westerly Place, purposely avoiding him, if he guessed right.

Had his sudden departure sealed his fate? Would he never have the chance to spend time alone with Verrick Grant? He had to admit the way she furnished her sunroom was a shock. It had triggered dark terrors from somewhere deep in his subconscious. But after giving it some thought, there must be some reasonable explanation. The dentist who filled his tooth was gentle and caring, even if a little unconventional. Once he'd gotten over his initial surprise, he had to admit the whips and chains in her sun room weren't consistent with the soothing, considerate woman he observed walking on the beach, tending her mother, or playing tooth fairy at a charity ball.

Doctor Grant bedevilled his senses. The woman was a mystery; both warm and friendly and at the same time, distant and aloof. The woman was a puzzle he wanted to solve.

He paced out the distance between his property stakes and envisioned the home he was going to build. It was strange how his neighbor haunted his thoughts, even out here in the wooded countryside. He thought of her with every stroke of his pen on the blueprints of the house. It was as though he was designing it with her in mind.

The mysterious Verrick Grant presented a challenge.

And Lionel Parford never backed down from a challenge.

Try as she might, Verrick couldn't keep from encountering Lionel Parford forever. It was embarrassing what he must think of her after seeing that film set in her starlight ballroom. She wasn't prepared to face him yet. But her avoidance tactics had run out. He was right behind her as she stepped into the elevator on her way to work Friday morning.

He looked his usual self—stunningly handsome, confident and completely in control. He unnerved her. Her pulse raced, her stomach fluttered, and she wanted to flee. It was hard to face someone who thought you enjoyed inflicting pain.

Verrick wished she'd left a few minutes earlier and avoided standing beside this man with golden hair and eyes as inviting as morning coffee. She shifted her weight from one foot to the other. The elevator ride had never taken so long nor been so tense.

Her neighbor seemed unaffected by the strained atmosphere.

He had the advantage of seeing her first, walking behind her, noticing the gentle sway of her hips and those fantastic legs that never escaped his attention. Had she but known it, he was eager to break down the barrier between them but had second thoughts when he stepped into the elevator beside her, felt the tension, and saw the anguished look on her face.

Did she find him so unbearable? Her eyes were wide with a hint of panic. She avoided looking at him and pursed her lips, refusing to be the first to speak.

He drank in the sight, surprised how happy he was to see her but baffled by her reaction. There was so little time to express what was on his mind as the elevator sped down to the main floor.

His cool, controlled exterior gave no hint of the turmoil inside. He inclined his head and waited for her to look at him. When she did, he nodded politely and acknowledged her presence in a business-like voice, "Doctor Grant."

She didn't flash that dazzling smile or change into the guise of the tooth fairy. To his dismay, anxious to make her escape, she replied equally as polite, "Mister Parford," silently thankful that her voice didn't squeak or her knees buckle.

The elevator glided smoothly to a stop, the doors swished open, and Verrick hurried to her car. Thankfully, for once it started without coaxing, and she shot out of the underground parking lot without a backward glance.

A disappointed Lionel Parford was left staring after the retreating rear bumper of her car, feeling saddened that the beguiling Doctor Grant couldn't get away from him fast enough.

"That's our last appointment today." Karen straightened Dr. Grant's examining room, putting the fluffy rabbit on the shelf beside Mr. Cuddles and the other stuffed toys. "I never thought I'd see Janie Connor willingly walk into the examining room and sit through a dental checkup."

"You prefer the terror-stricken cases?"

"Oh no. Mrs. Connor told me Janie screamed the place down, the last dentist she went to. I like to see the children relaxed. But . . ."

"But . . . what?"

Karen grinned. "I love seeing you in action with the difficult cases. It's like being in the theatre not in a dentist office."

"Did you have any particular patient in mind?"

"I told my husband about Mr. Parford and we laughed through dinner. You had the man so disoriented, you could have amputated his leg without him noticing."

"Don't remind me. The man lives in the same building as I do—he's my neighbor. I'm having trouble keeping my composure when I run into him. He thinks I'm a crazed sadist."

"You did get a little crazy, threatening to shave off his mustache and all."

"Did I really?"

"You did."

Verrick groaned. "Once started, I got carried away." She shrugged. "We got the job done and he survived."

"Have you seen him since?"

"Only in the elevator this morning."

Karen stood silently waiting for all the details. "How did he react?"

"He gave me 'the look'."

"The look?"

Verrick shrugged, searching for the words to describe what had passed between them that morning. "You know the look you give a dog when you're trying to train him? You give a command then wait, and give him 'the look'." That's how it felt to her. He was expecting something and she didn't obey.

Karen nodded. "That bad, was it?"

"That bad! I think he's keeping his distance, afraid I'll attack him with drills and clamps and weapons of torture."

"Did he swat you with a rolled-up newspaper?"

"No . . . but I'm sure he wanted to."

Karen's thoughtful voice gave Verrick something to consider. "He didn't know you're a dentist. It came as a shock. Men don't like being caught off guard, it makes them uncomfortable. My husband hates surprises. He likes to feel in control."

Verrick agreed. "You have a good point. I don't think Mr. Parford appreciates surprises either."

Karen reached for her coat. "Give him time. He'll get over it. Even my husband admits he's not always right."

As she tucked the woolly scarf around her neck, Verrick shook her head. "I'm not so sure about Mr. Parford. I think he'll consider me a lunatic until the day he dies."

The two women were ready to leave the office when Karen asked, "Have you time to stop for tea before heading home? My husband is working late tonight and I wanted to check out a new cafe I saw advertised. It's close—just over on Russell Avenue."

"I'd love to. What's the place called?"

"The Dream Cafe."

"Sounds romantic."

"The owner had a dream to open a restaurant. Afternoon tea is a specialty."

Verrick was glad of an excuse to avoid Westerly Place and another chance encounter with her neighbor.

The restaurant was a cozy mix of East and West, green plaid drapes and tablecloths, a large oak bar, decorated archways, intimate banquets and private tables with oak chairs.

The menu listed a selection of teas and coffees, cookies, sandwiches and desserts.

Karen pointed to her menu. "What do you suppose this is—Bubble Tea with Pearls from Taiwan?"

"Sounds interesting whatever it is. I think I'll play it safe and have the Strawberry Tea."

Before the waitress delivered their order, another couple entered the cafe, the woman definitely in the last months of her pregnancy. Verrick looked up into the smiling face of Gavin Parford.

"Verrick Grant. How lovely to see you again."

The young woman beside him was looking at Verrick with a friendly smile, as if they were already well acquainted and best friends. Come to think of it, she did look familiar, not one of her patients, but she would remember if they had met.

Gavin Parford settled the confusion. "Allow me to introduce my sister, Rachel."

Of course, Verrick chided herself, they're twins. No wonder she looks familiar.

Rachel was not at all like her older brother. She was bubbly and eager to sit down and get acquainted with the woman who had Lion swooning in that poster Gavin had given her. "Do you mind if we join you?" Rachel's warm brown eyes were so kindly, Karen and Verrick were glad to have her join them.

"This is my assistant, Karen Taylor." She gestured to the

couple now seated across from them. "Gavin Parford and his sister Rachel . . ."

"Mickelson," she filled in.

Karen's eyebrows rose, alerted by the name Parford. She couldn't hold back her curiosity. "Are you related to Lionel Parford?"

Gavin was surprised by such interest. Had Lion already roared at all the young women in White Rock? "Yes, he's our older brother."

Karen suppressed a fit of giggles as the waitress interrupted, placing the fragrant steaming Strawberry Tea in front of Verrick and a tall fluted glass with a bamboo straw in front of Karen. The tea was served cold and some pearls (chewy giant bits of something like tapioca) were on the bottom of the glass. Karen took an adventurous sip, then smiled, and declared, "Delicious."

Gavin and Rachel gave their orders then both turned their attention on Karen. "Our brother has only lived in White Rock a few months and he isn't known for being sociable. How did you manage to meet him?"

"He had a tooth filled last week. I'm Dr. Grant's assistant."

Two pair of astonished brown eyes stared at Verrick. A bomb could have been dropped at their feet, they looked so shocked.

"Doctor Grant?" they repeated in unison; their faces beaming and their voices incredulous.

Verrick calmly sipped her tea and sampled the cake served with it.

Gavin was grinning from ear to ear. "Let me get this straight. Are you saying that Verrick is a dentist?"

Karen nodded. "She's the best, specializes in children and trauma patients."

Rachel burst out laughing. "That's unbelievable. Lion steers clear of dentists. They horrify him." She didn't give voice to her thoughts that her big brother didn't look the least bit horrified as he held the tooth fairy in his arms at the Halloween ball.

Verrick nodded her agreement and answered in a somber voice that unknowingly revealed her regrets, "That accurately describes our relationship—he's horrified."

Gavin suspected that was far from the truth. His brother may be mystified, enchanted, even smitten, but he wasn't quaking in fear. He never quaked in fear. Before he could gather his thoughts to speak, Karen began describing the dentist visit to Rachel.

"She threatened to shave off his mustache. I thought he was ready to have a heart attack, then she gave him a teddy bear to hold and told him to floss carefully. Just like safe sex, one must never take chances."

Rachel laughed. "She didn't dare!"

"She did. I was trying to keep the tooth well suctioned but I wanted to laugh so badly, tears were streaming down my cheeks."

Gavin looked at Verrick, resigned to the fact the whole world was going to hear about Mr. Parford's visit to her dentist chair. "You threatened to shave off his mustache?"

"Apparently I did."

"Lion would never sit still for that. He's always been so proud of that mustache; it's his symbol of manhood and authority. Did you have him tied to the chair?"

Verrick gave him a quelling look and the tooth fairy voice sweetly replied, "Mr. Parford was a good boy. He hugged Mr. Cuddles as instructed and needed no restraints."

Rachel was laughing so hard she had to put her teacup back in its saucer before her shaking hand had it spilled all over the tablecloth.

"Did you pat him on the head and give him a lollipop?"

"Oh no, Rachel. Mr. Molar doesn't like lollipops."

Karen whispered to Rachel who obviously had never seen Verrick play-acting before, "Dr. Grant gives them a package of nuts and tells them to chew well and brush after eating."

"Nuts . . ." Rachel burbled through her laughter, "how fitting!" She put her hand on her extended abdomen. The laughter had set her baby to kicking and she could feel the thumps against her hand. "Even Baby is anxious to meet the brave dentist able to subdue Uncle Lionel."

Verrick smiled at Rachel, secretly envying her upcoming motherhood. "I'd love to meet your baby . . . but wait until three years of age before coming to my office."

Gavin was sipping his tea with a look of disbelief. "You're really a dentist?" Who'd have thought the babe next door to Lionel did the only kind of work his big brother detested?

"I really am," Verrick confirmed. "Just ask your brother. He cringes at the sight of me and avoids me like the plague."

Karen was slurping the Pearls from the bottom of her glass through the bamboo straw. She chewed them thoughtfully and smiled. "My husband will never believe I drank a glass of cold tea with gluck in the bottom. I hate it when he dunks cookies in his coffee and there's a mass of crumbs stuck in the bottom of the cup."

"I know what you mean," Rachel sympathized.

Karen looked at her watch, said her farewells and excused herself. She wanted to drive home before the rush hour traffic was too bad. As she walked to her car, she mulled the fact that Lionel Parford's brother and sister seemed so very friendly and easy-going, nothing like their older brother. They called him Lion—the name suited, regal, and untamed.

Verrick sat a little longer with her neighbor's younger siblings. "What brings the two of you to White Rock today?"

"George doesn't want me driving this far along in my pregnancy, so when Gavin said he was delivering some plants to Lion, I insisted on coming. I'm getting cabin fever being confined to the house."

Gavin grimaced at his sister. "I thought I was rid of her when she got married."

Verrick watched the banter between these two very similar looking twins, enjoying the teasing between brother and sister.

"What are you growing in your sunroom, Verrick?"

"Not a thing. It seems just right for plants but I'm no green thumb. My friend named it my starlight ballroom. I have yet to think up a use for it."

"Gavin is a landscape architect, if you want plants, let him help."

"Thanks . . . but . . ."

Gavin smiled with understanding. "I'd be glad to offer advice but don't feel pressured. Indoor plants take a lot of tending, watering, spraying, fertilizing and still they don't always flourish. I thought Lion should put a hot tub and sauna in his sunroom but he wanted greenery. Take your time deciding." His grin was contagious. "I can get you a deal on a hot tub."

Rachel excused herself to use the bathroom.

Not one for subtlety, Gavin got right to the information he most wanted to know. "Truthfully, Verrick, how are things between you and Lion? I could have sworn big brother was interested, is there really a cold war on the fourth floor of Westerly Place?"

Verrick's downcast eyes said more than her words. "I saw him in the elevator this morning. I'd say relations are chilled. I don't think he appreciated finding out what I do for a living the way he did. We do our best to avoid each other."

Gavin slowly shook his head. "Lion is a great actor. He never lets on when something's bothering him. He suffers in silence. We all had him to run to when we were upset, but he's the oldest and always had to be strong and invincible." He patted Verrick's hand where it lay on the table.

"Don't be fooled, when he seems distant may be when he's most interested. Lion thinks up the most devious plans."

Verrick dismissed this with a flick of her hand. "No, Gavin, I don't think your brother is interested. My mother once told me, 'Good fences make good neighbors.' Your brother and I live in the same building . . . behind fences. Perhaps that's best. You wouldn't want to hear there'd been a murder at Westerly Place."

She said this with such feeling, Gavin didn't dare argue with her. He knew she had misjudged Lionel and said with sympathy, "That bad is it?"

Rachel caught the last bit of the conversation as she returned to the table. "What's that bad?"

"Verrick and Lion being next-door neighbors."

Rachel squeezed Verrick's hand. "Lion can be a beast, can't he?" She didn't give Verrick a chance to reply. "He's so good at everything, sometimes we wondered if he wasn't a robot. Gavin and I teased him mercilessly and he was always a good sport about it. He never held a grudge. When I look back on all those years, I realize we couldn't have had a better big brother."

Verrick found that hard to believe. Mr. Parford was so controlled. She couldn't imagine getting an emotional reaction out of him, although he did look ready to strangle her when she had him in her dentist chair.

Gavin added his voice to his sister's argument. "Don't be put off by all that growling exterior. Behind it all is a flesh and blood man who can actually laugh at himself."

That was too much to take. Verrick choked on the very thought. "Mr. Perfect?" she croaked in disbelief.

The twins looked at each other and began to chuckle in unison. "What did you just call Lion?"

"Mr. Perfect," Verrick repeated.

"That's what we called him when we were little. It made him furious."

"You don't call him that anymore?"

"Oh no, not for a long time. It took us a while, but we

saw how kind and human he really was. He has feelings as intense as we do. He just keeps them hidden."

"What changed your opinion?"

"It wasn't any one thing," Rachel pondered the question. "But I remember the day our dog was run over by a car. We cried and Lionel hugged us both. When I looked up, there were tears in his eyes. That's when I knew for sure he wasn't a robot."

Gavin thrust in the final comment. "Give the guy a break, Verrick. Being that reliable is hard on a guy . . . and it gets mighty lonely."

Verrick didn't realize she was being worked over by two expert conspirators. She didn't say anything, but it was obvious she was thinking over their words.

Rachel winked at Gavin while Verrick stood to leave and buttoned up her coat. Their mother had cautioned them about playing Cupid, but sometimes their stubborn brother needed a little help.

Verrick smiled at the brother and sister. "It was nice to have met you Rachel." Her somber expression confirmed that the purposely-placed comments had hit their mark.

She was barely through the door before Gavin thumped his sister on the back. "You're a devious woman. I hope your baby knows what he's getting himself in for. That dog story was the best!"

Rachel's smug grin said it all. "Sometimes Lion needs a little help. What are sisters for?"

Gavin choked on that. "He'll kill us if he finds out."

A melancholy gloom settled over Verrick as she drove home through the cold rain of a late November afternoon. Her heart ached for a home and loving family. She envied the Parford twins. Her car sloshed through the wet streets. She once thought loving families only existed in works of fiction but she knew differently now.

As she swerved into her parking spot, she admitted the fact—she was getting broody, dreaming "happy families".

It happened every year about Christmas time. Verrick locked her car door and scolded herself. *You can't miss something you've never had, so stop making yourself miserable.* She took the elevator up to the fourth floor with a haunting sadness filling her. The bright Christmas decorations she'd seen in the shops only served to remind her how alone she was as the holiday season approached. It wasn't like her to be this glum.

Drat that man! He looks so good, does everything to perfection and has the kind of family I'd die for. Some things are not fair!

She slammed her door and stomped off to stand under a hot shower until she felt the tension ease and the pangs of envy give way to feelings of thankfulness for her good health, fine home, good friends, and a job she loved.

She was wrapped in her terry cloth bathrobe rubbing her hair dry when the telephone started ringing and jolted her back to reality.

"Verrick, you sound funny. Are you all right?"

"I'm fine, Jenna. Still dripping, just out of the shower."

"Have I got a deal for you, girl. You'll love it."

"Uh, oh. Already I don't like the sound of it."

"Now, now. Wait until you hear this." Jenna didn't give Verrick a chance to refuse before she'd heard her out. "The fairy in the Christmas pantomime has taken ill and they need a replacement immediately. I thought of you instantly. You're perfect for the role."

"I'm not convinced, Jenna. Explain it to me. What exactly is a Christmas pantomime?"

"It's like a fairy tale but the male lead is played by a woman and the female lead is played by a man."

"Weird. You mean it's a play done in drag?"

"No, no, nothing like that. It's all in good fun, not just for the children, for the whole family."

"It sounds strange to me. Isn't it more your style of thing? Why don't you take the part?"

"It runs through the whole month of December and

Ralph's parents have invited us to spend Christmas with them in Kelowna. I couldn't be there for every performance. You have to do it Verrick, you're the only one. And you'll have fun, I promise."

"I don't know, Jenna. I haven't been on stage since high school and it's such short notice. You say performances start in less than two weeks—I can't learn a role in so little time."

"You're a natural for the part, it won't take any preparation at all. They need a good fairy to open the play, explain the story and help the hero when things look bleak. You enter on a puff of smoke, wave your magic wand and glitter about the stage. The children love it. None of the little ones get scared because they know the good fairy will make things right."

"It sounds easy enough. But why me?"

"The elderly woman who's played the part for the past many years had a stroke last week. It's a last minute emergency to fill her role. Verrick, you can't disappoint a theater full of children, not at Christmas time." Jenna crossed her fingers. If nothing else, that plea to Verrick's soft spot for children should work.

"Okay. I'll give it a try. When can I meet the director and attend a rehearsal?"

"I knew you wouldn't let those children down. Tonight, eight o'clock at the White Rock Playhouse on Johnston Road. Thanks, Verrick. You won't regret this."

Verrick hung up the telephone and wondered about the wisdom of playing Fairy Snowflake in the Christmas pantomime. True, she could play a fairy easily enough, but that part about cross-dressing had her shaking her head.

She had no plans to visit either of her parents this Christmas. Being in a play would keep her too busy to feel lonely or dream about the perfect families gathered around their Christmas trees celebrating the holiday. Christmas was one time of year she regretted being an only child with much-married parents—no family gatherings, no holiday traditions repeated year after year, no feeling of belonging. She vigorously rubbed her hair dry. Yes, playing Fairy Snowflake was a good idea. It would keep her mind off all she was missing.

Verrick found the White Rock Playhouse easily. A final dress rehearsal was in full swing, a boisterous opening musical number with a brightly-costumed chorus ranging from small children to grandparents. The joyful enthusiasm won her heart immediately. The players obviously knew each other well, they worked together like one large happy family.

The director greeted her with open arms. "You're a godsend." He thrust a typed script into her hands, aimed her toward the costume co-ordinator and gave her no chance for second thoughts. "Try on your costume and we'll run through your lines."

Swept up in the excitement, Verrick didn't argue. She slipped into the glittery fairy gown which needed a great many tucks and gathers, picked up her wand and rapidly scanned her lines as the seamstress hemmed and stitched to make the dress small enough to fit her female curves.

"Ready?" the director shouted.

"Ready," Verrick nodded.

A blast of smoke from behind the scenes and she stumbled on stage. Somewhere her glasses had been misplaced and she peered shortsightedly beyond the stage lights into the audience—a murky blur to her unfocused eyes.

"Keep that in," the director chortled. "I love it—a shortsighted fairy!"

Verrick delivered her speech, opening the play, explaining the story for the benefit of both adults and children. Her quiet voice drew the audience in. There was a noticeable hush amongst the cast and crew sitting in the theater. The woman had talent.

When she paused, swept her wand to encompass the audience and strained to look out into the sea of blurred faces, it was as though she had made eye contact with every single one of the onlookers. Her question was barely above a whisper. "Do you believe in fairies?"

The enthusiastic response came in a roar. "Yes!"

The director and producer nodded. "She's a winner. Two minutes and she has the audience in her hands. We have ourselves a new Christmas fairy."

Verrick tumbled into bed exhausted but happy. She patted the golden lion beside her pillow. "I'm going to enjoy this Christmas."

Chapter Seven

J enna smiled into the phone. "Verrick, I wouldn't miss opening night for the world. Ralph and I have aisle seats in the third row, Darren, too. I can't wait. It sounds hilarious."

"It is, Jenna. I just hope I don't giggle. My role is small. Any longer on the stage and I'd surely lose my composure and laugh out loud. The dame is a riot."

"Are you sorry I talked you talked you into this?"

"No, never. The cast is like a family, local people, all ages. It's delightful, Jenna. I was worried about spending my first Christmas alone here in White Rock. Two weeks ago, I didn't know what a pantomime was but now I'm glad to be part of it."

"How about dinner at your place? The performance doesn't start till eight, what time do you have to be at the playhouse?"

"Not until seven."

"That'll work out fine. We can stay and clear up after dinner and you can rush off and turn into Fairy Snowflake. We'll arrive in time for the grand opening."

"I have a roast to put in the oven, you bring dessert. Shall I make arrangements with Darren or do you want to?"

"You call him, Verrick. It may be his last chance to see you before he moves."

"I'll do it, Jenna. See you tomorrow around six o'clock."

The calendar turned to December but still Lionel Parford had no luck getting near his neighbor. She was out every evening; he saw her car race off regularly about seven o'clock. Did she keep avoiding him because she had a busy night life or did she have some rule about not socializing with patients?

The woman puzzled him and he couldn't get her out of his mind. He rubbed his jaw as he slid his car into his parking space. Perhaps it was gratitude that his mouth was pain free, no throbbing misery at the touch of hot coffee or stabbing pain from the chill of ice cream. Only now did he realize how often in the past he cringed in agony from aching teeth; only now after Verrick Grant had changed all that. He tried to convince himself the reason she crept into his thoughts with regularity was gratitude, nothing more.

He frowned as he caught the red glow of her tail lights sweeping out of the parking garage. He slammed his car door with unusual force before locking it, then scowled fiercely as he headed to the stairs.

He stomped up three flights in a foul temper. That Mercedes was parked in front of Westerly Place as he drove into the underground parking. Had the guy taken up residence in her apartment? Why was he still here when Verrick was out?

He threw his briefcase down in his hallway and yanked open the closet to hang up his overcoat. If the woman is engaged or involved with the driver of that pretentious car, why doesn't she come out and say so?

That would explain why she avoided any attempt he made to get near her.

He hadn't spent two seconds with her since that day in her dentist's office, only that chilling greeting in the elevator.

He glowered down into the street at the offending Mercedes.

Even Gavin and Rachel had seen more of his elusive neighbor than he had.

Opening night was a success. The dame was outrageous, the chorus sang beautifully, the actors remembered their lines, and the fairy stole the show. The audience felt such sympathy for her short-sighted bumblings, they cheered her on. Verrick could pick out Jenna's voice, and Ralph's, too, when she asked the audience if they believed in fairies. Darren was a little more conservative, he frowned on childish displays, but she heard him chuckling at the off-color remarks of the cross-dressing dame.

And so, Verrick's days fell into a pattern. She was a dentist by day and Fairy Snowflake by night. There was a matinee on Sunday and no performance on Monday.

Keeping busy was a wonderful antidote to the twinges of sadness. She often got weepy around Christmas time. It was an emotional time of year but this Christmas she had no time to feel sorry for herself or think about the neighbor who thought she was a ghoul.

That woman is impossible. She makes herself invisible, unavailable, never at home, always on the go. She could have moved out for as often as her car is in its parking space. Lionel Parford was fuming to himself as he drove home to Westerly Place on Monday evening. Verrick Grant had successfully avoided any contact with him for weeks and he was furious, as much with himself as with her.

He shouldn't have bolted from her apartment so abruptly without giving her some explanation. But the sight of that torturer's chamber in her sunroom had awakened some deep inner fear he was embarrassed to admit still lingered within him. He thought those dentist nightmares were left in the past along with his childhood. In the calm light of day, he could see he acted irrationally and he wanted to apologize. But the impossible woman didn't give him a chance, she didn't accept personal calls at her office and she was never home.

Had she eloped with the driver of that Mercedes? The thought made him irritable; he was grinding his teeth and scowling as he swerved rapidly into the entrance to the underground parking.

His eyes opened wide and a faint smile softened the angry look on his face. Her car was parked in its spot, spattered with mud, its rear bumper dented and in need of a good wash. It was a beautiful sight.

Lionel Parford loped up the four flights of stairs two at a time, only slightly breathless as he reached the penthouse floor. He wasn't leaving anything to chance. Verrick Grant wasn't going to slip out on him before he had an opportunity to talk to her. Briefcase still in hand, not daring to let her escape, he knocked on the door of 401.

The aroma of roasting chicken with sage tempted his taste buds as a surprised Verrick opened the door. She was barefoot wearing well-worn corduroy jeans that hugged her shapely bottom and a bulky pink sweater. Obviously she wasn't expecting company, her hair was uncombed and wildly curling across her forehead and tumbling over her shoulders; her face was freshly scrubbed free of makeup and her big blue eyes were filled with questions as she studied her uninvited guest.

Lionel Parford, always in control, never at a loss for words, never caught unawares, stood speechless on her doorstep and swallowed her with his eyes.

It seemed like ages since he'd seen her, he couldn't get his fill. The woman was natural and unassuming; he found her ravishing. Add to that the delicious smells of something wonderful cooking in her kitchen, and his stomach clenched, a hungry feeling overwhelming him.

Monday, the one evening of the week without a pantomime performance, was when Verrick cooked, counting on leftovers to heat up quickly before dashing to the theatre all the rest of the week. Only moments ago she wondered if she should invite someone to share all this food as she'd gone overboard, craving a properly-cooked meal and prepared enough to keep her in leftovers for a month. The smile she gave her neighbor was welcoming, something he was unprepared for. Once again, Lionel Parford was thrown off guard.

"Mr. Parford. How nice to see you. Won't you come in?"

Lionel stepped into her hallway, aware for the first time he was still clutching his briefcase. He was here to explain his hasty departure, but she made it difficult. No woman should look that good in old clothing ready for the rag bin and no food should smell so scrumptious when he was standing here with an empty stomach.

Verrick didn't notice her neighbor was tongue-tied, she was preoccupied with the pots on her stovetop. "Excuse me one minute, I have something cooking in the kitchen."

He didn't have to be told that, he was lightheaded from the heavenly aroma. Automatically, he set his briefcase down in the hall and followed her into the kitchen. As yet, he hadn't spoken a word.

She was draining water from the cooked potatoes and motioned to a steaming pot on the stove. "Will you turn the heat off under those carrots?" Lionel immediately turned off the burner and carried the pot to the sink, drained them and added a pat of butter, just the way he liked them.

"Thanks. I hate overcooked vegetables. I like them a bit crisp, not soggy."

He finally found his voice. "My thoughts exactly."

Verrick pulled the roast chicken out of the oven and set it on the cutting board. Then she stuck a fork into an apple crisp, decided it was fully cooked and placed it on the sideboard to cool.

Without warning, she turned to her visitor and said, "Are you free for dinner Mr. Parford? I'm ready to sit down and eat and you're welcome to join me."

He didn't stop to think. "Yes, I'm free. I'd be delighted to accept your invitation. And my name is Lionel."

She smiled, too hungry for idle chatter. "Good. Put that chicken on a platter, and spoon the stuffing into this dish. I'll make gravy and get the vegetables into serving bowls." She gestured toward the dining room. "Add another place setting and we're ready to eat."

She was comfortable in a kitchen, obviously an accomplished cook. He hadn't suspected a domestic side, although the way she'd furnished her apartment was cozy and home-like. He should have guessed cooking was another of her skills.

Verrick opened the refrigerator and handed him a chilled bottle of white wine. "Here . . . Lionel. You open this and I'll carry things through to the dining room. I'm starving. I hope you're hungry, too. Sometimes I get carried away in the kitchen."

That's not the only place you get carried away, he silently commented to himself. He was still reeling from her performance in the dentist office.

Verrick thought the massive amount of food cooked for herself alone was the reason for the strange look directed at her. It must look greedy from his well-mannered point of view. Too bad, she shrugged to herself as she placed the warm bread rolls on the table. I haven't had a home-cooked meal all week and I won't let anyone spoil my enjoyment of this one.

She looked down at the carving knife in her hand and up at the odd look on his face. She grinned and offered him the knife. "Perhaps you'd feel safer wielding this than seeing it in my hand."

He accepted the knife and returned her grin, then sliced the chicken with the skill of a professional chef. He really was too good to be true. When Verrick carved a chicken there were crumbles and odd-shaped bits.

Any thoughts of conversation vanished as they served themselves vegetables, buttered rolls, sipped wine, and began to eat, savoring the subtle flavors, tasting and enjoying and taking second helpings. Only when the hollow emptiness inside was satisfied, did Verrick acknowledge her guest. "So, Lionel, what brought you to my door this evening?"

In spite of his impeccable table manners, he looked rather dazed. He didn't answer her question right away but said instead, "This is delicious." She knew his praise was sincere because a few skeletal remains were all that were left of the once plump bird. The vegetable dishes had fared little better, only a few spoonfuls remained in each.

"Don't tell me you smelled dinner cooking and tried your luck for an invitation."

"No. The venting system doesn't allow cooking odors into the hallway." She couldn't tell if that look on his face was serious or if he was teasing her. He hid a lot behind that mustache.

"I had no idea you were a marvelous cook. The last thing I tasted at your hand was piña colada and that was an experience I wasn't anxious to repeat." Then he smiled at her, a full smile that even his mustache couldn't disguise. "I never properly thanked you for fixing my tooth. It was painless and has remained so ever since. I can't thank you enough."

His probing look brought back that jittery feeling. "All in a day's work." She was glad he didn't hold a grudge. According to Karen, she'd been pretty outrageous. She hadn't expected him to thank her for it.

But he wasn't finished yet. "I beg to differ. It was an exceptional piece of work, a master performance." He blinked, as though coming to his senses from a long way away, surveyed the paltry remains on the table and blessed her with a glorious smile that spread all the way up to his chocolate brown eyes. "Three weeks ago I couldn't believe I'd willingly eat dinner with a dentist. The thought sent shivers down my spine."

Warmed by his smile, Verrick didn't take offense. "We dentists are human, too."

He swivelled in his chair to catch a glimpse of her sunroom. It was entirely empty, dim evening light reflecting off the bare wood floor. Verrick saw the direction of his glance and laughed.

It was contagious. His deep laughter blended with hers. They both began to speak at the same time. "I apologize . . ."

"Me first," Verrick rushed on. "I apologize for not explaining about that gruesome scene in my sunroom . . ."

"I didn't give you a chance. I was so startled, I bolted for the exit without a backward glance. I apologize, I wasn't thinking; some deep buried terror surfaced, adrenaline began pumping, and the urge to flee was undeniable."

"Apology accepted." Her melodic voice was warm and accepting, he no longer felt the need to explain. She understood. He relaxed and basked her in a heart-stopping smile that whisked away all thoughts of teeth from her professional dentist's mind. It was an effort to make her voice respond. "Would you like an explanation for that scene in the sunroom?"

"Only if you'd like to give it . . ."

Verrick got up from her chair and pushed it into the table. "You light the fireplace. I'll make coffee and bring in dessert. Then you'll get your explanation."

He watched her pad barefoot into the kitchen. Such a soothing person to share a meal with, no fancy dress or flirtation, no tittering laughter or drawing attention to herself. Yes, Verrick Grant was the sort of woman he'd love to come home to every evening. He knelt before the fireplace, arranged paper, kindling and logs from the basket beside the hearth, then struck a match to start the fire. His first meeting with his neighbor flashed through his mind— the smoke alarm and her dishevelled appearance. He found her attractive, even then.

Fortunately, Verrick had her glasses on and none of the

coffee grounds spilled onto the hot burner. She served the steaming apple crisp with vanilla ice cream melting in creamy rivulets over the top. As she carried the dessert tray to the living room, a fire was blazing (and no smoke alarm was sending its shrill warning above the quiet crackle of logs in the fireplace).

She sat beside him on the sofa, her bare feet stretched out to capture the heat of the flames. There was no need for chatter. They enjoyed the warm apple crisp fragrant with cinnamon and the smooth chill of ice cream on the tongue.

Her wistful expression caught his attention. "Having trouble coming up with an explanation? It's all right if you don't want to tell me."

Verrick grinned. "No, nothing like that. It's very simple. My friend Jenna works in the movie industry as a locations manager. She used my sunroom as a set for a small scene in some horror movie involving a strange doctor with an unusual private life. Simple as that. It was a movie set meant to send shivers down your spine. Jenna did a great job, didn't she?"

She sat with her feet curled under her on the sofa, the soft light of the fire casting a glow over her gentle face with the delicious smile. He could almost taste those delectable lips. With firm resolve, he pulled back his cloak of aloof dignity. "Indeed. She set *my* nerves on edge."

"Would you like more coffee?"

"Yes." Before she could move, he added, "I'll get it. You stay where you are—you look comfortable."

But she was uncomfortable. Everything about him was still perfect . . . but now she found herself beginning to like it. She couldn't use it as an excuse to avoid him much longer. She liked the way he lit the fire without filling the room with smoke . . . and she liked the way he was so considerate . . . and who could find fault with a man who knew his way around the kitchen? Well, he should shouldn't he, he designed it, and what's more he lives in one exactly the same. And he was such reassuring company, no fuss or pretense. He was disturbing. She was beginning to like him far too much.

Lionel didn't want this evening to end. He drank another cup of coffee he didn't really need, watching Verrick gaze into the fire and smiled at the irony of the situation. That was his dentist he was mooning over. Unbelievable! Only weeks ago he'd suffer agonies to avoid contact with a dentist.

She looked sleepy and vulnerable as she sat in the warmth of the fire. It was time to return to his own suite but he didn't want this truce to be called off the instant he left.

"The yacht club has a Christmas sail past this Saturday." Her questioning gaze urged him to continue. "They sail from Crescent Beach and Blaine past the White Rock breakwater. Even Santa Claus arrives by boat. The children are given treats, carolers sing, the ocean is lit with decorated boats, and a good time is had by all, or so I'm told." He paused, uncertain of her response. "Will you view the sail past and join me for dinner afterward?"

Verrick turned at the sound of his voice, staring into those soulful brown eyes. "I would love to see the sail past. What time does it begin?"

"Five o'clock."

"Good. I can come but I'll have to skip dinner. I have . . . a previous commitment that evening. I must be home by seven o'clock."

Lionel Parford smiled but it was a very somber one. He was surprisingly disappointed. He wanted to cook dinner for her. He envied the lucky guy taking her out at seven.

He stood to his full height beside the sofa and stretched out his hands to assist her to her feet. "I look forward to Saturday evening." He kept her hand in his as they walked to the door, where he stopped and looked down into her eyes. "Thank you again for the lovely dinner." He took both her hands in his and lowered his head to kiss her, very thoroughly. She was glad he had hold of her hands—she felt in danger of crumbling at the knees and melting into a puddle on the carpet. He lifted his head, applied a gentle pressure to her hands, then bent to retrieve his briefcase, reached for the door handle and let himself out.

Verrick exhaled a deep sigh and stared at the closed door. She felt light-headed and quivery all over. *I've been overdoing things lately*, she told herself, *working all day and at the theater until past ten o'clock every night*. She turned toward her bedroom and almost floated across the carpet. *A good night's sleep is what I need. I'll be back to my old self by morning.*

The golden lion sitting on her bed differed with that opinion. She would dream of a Lion and that quivery feeling would persist.

Some things could not be cured by a good night's sleep.

The stylishly-dressed woman in the latest fashion breezed right past Mrs. Ross' desk without bothering to greet her, or ask to be announced in Mr. Parford's office.

Mrs. Ross glowered at the offensive woman's back. *Laureen Geddis is rude and pampered. Let Mr. Parford deal with her. It's not my fault I didn't buzz through and warn him. What he sees in that woman is beyond me.*

"Lion, darling. Surprise! I thought I'd come and steal you away for lunch." She trilled this message in a high-pitched breathy voice while flashing a much-practiced smile at the man studiously bent over his drafting table.

From the scowl on his face, it was obvious she was interrupting a session of work he was deeply involved in. This didn't deter Laureen Geddis. She was used to getting her own way and confident her charms could distract any man from work, even Lionel Parford.

His voice was calm and controlled, but had she been perceptive enough to look, Miss Geddis would have seen the sparks of anger in his deep brown eyes. "Hello, Laureen. You've caught me at a busy time. I want to complete these blueprints before the weekend."

The girlish laughter wasn't becoming in a woman in her thirties, an annoying fact Lionel Parford noticed with pursed lips and a withering glare.

Miss Geddis was far from being withered. She tottered across the carpet in her high-heeled shoes and stood close behind Lionel, purposely brushing against his arm as she bent over to study the work in progress in front of him.

"What an old-fashioned house! No wonder you're struggling over these plans. They must be deadly boring to work on. You need a break, Lion. Take me out someplace nice for lunch. Then you can come back to these dull plans." She glanced scathingly over the blueprints spread out on the massive table. "Who wants to build a dreary, unexciting, old-fashioned house like this anyway?" She giggled and leaned in closer to the man looking at her with a cool reserve his younger siblings knew meant trouble. "Whoever wants a house like this belongs in the dark ages."

"Is that right?" the deep voice replied without emotion.

"Of course it's right, Lion. Just look at these drawings. No one lives in a place like that anymore, not since the first settlers homesteaded the prairies. It's a farm house— no sophistication, no style, no walls of glass or skylights, no sea view. It isn't grand or luxurious, not suitable for throwing parties. Just look at it—not even a swimming pool."

She put her hands on her hips and stated boldly, "I wouldn't live in a place like this if you paid me!" She was wound up to go on at length, but Lionel Parford cut her short.

"Luckily, you won't be asked to."

"Now Lion, don't be touchy. You needn't speak to me in that tone of voice. I'm not the client who's asked you to design this silly house. Forget about it and come for lunch."

"I'm sorry, Laureen. I'm working."

"Don't be a stick-in-the-mud Lion. Surely you can spare time for me." She sucked in her breath and posed provocatively. "You can't tell me those plans are more important than I am."

Lionel Parford looked her up and down insolently, then drawled, "The plans are more important, Laureen."

"You'll regret this, Lion!"

She squared her shoulders and stomped out of the office, slamming the door with enough force to rattle the pens on Mrs. Ross' desk.

Without so much as a nod or any acknowledgment of the secretary's presence, the angry woman fled the offices of the architectural firm.

Mrs. Ross couldn't suppress the sigh of relief and the pleased smile that spread across her face.

Three cheers for Mr. Parford. He finally put that nasty woman in her place. About time, too.

Saturday dawned frosty cold with a brisk wind off the water. Verrick figured it would be great for sailboats but the people standing on the pier would freeze to death. She rummaged through her drawers for her warmest sweater, wool socks and heavy slacks.

When Lionel Parford knocked on her door at five o'clock, she was bundled up under so many layers that she felt like a plump snowman. But that was not the impression her neighbor had. Her eyes sparkled with excitement, playful and vibrant, and he returned her smile, feeling more youthful and alive than he had in ages.

He took hold of her hand to guide her across the train tracks and kept it snugly in his own as they walked the length of the wooden pier, jostled in the crowds of people, children, and carol-singers making their way to the end. There the colored lights decorating several large sailboats were already in sight sailing across the dark water of the bay, like Christmas decorations bobbing on the cold sea.

Verrick leaned against the rail, watching the lines of gaily decorated boats approach. The chill wind tossed hair across her eyes but she brushed it back with her warmly-gloved hand. Lionel Parford stood close beside her, sheltering her from the blunt force of the sea breeze. The crowd had thickened and many children squealed in delight at the sight of the decorated boats. Verrick snuggled closer beside Lionel Parford to make room for two small girls beside the rail. His arm went around her waist and pulled her gently into his side.

Verrick luxuriated in the feeling of security and warmth. Here on a cold December night, in a chilling sea breeze, jostled by people on all sides, she felt protected and cherished. It made no sense. Children were rubbing their hands together and stomping their feet to keep warm, peering into the inky black water for the first sign of Santa Claus' boat but Verrick felt heated through even though the wind had colored her cheeks a rosy red and whipped her hair loose from under her hood. Lionel Parford was so calm and comforting, she felt happy as she lifted her face to look in the direction he was pointing.

A power boat, moving faster than the others around it, was heading for the dock, leaving a foaming wake behind. It was gaily lit with a huge Christmas tree on deck and Santa Claus himself, surrounded by elves, waving to the waiting children on the pier, calling out in his booming voice, "Merry Christmas!"

The joy on Verrick's face matched that on any of the excited children's. Lionel couldn't resist the full lips that smiled so unselfconsciously and tightened his hold around her waist, intending to lower his head. Just then, a high-pitched voice cried out, "Dr. Grant!" A small girl threw her arms around Verrick and hugged her. She slipped out of Lionel Parford's grasp, knelt down, and returned the hug.

"Hello Linda. Are you here to welcome Santa Claus, too?"

"Yes. He brings candy canes."

Lionel Parford watched her giving full attention to the small child, genuinely attentive, unconcerned with the people milling about or her soft wool scarf dragging on the wet boards of the pier. And how remarkable a child would come up and hug her dentist. At that age he would run a mile to avoid such an encounter. How different her patients were from the terrified child he was. Verrick Grant could charm bears out of their caves, she was that endearing.

The loud clang of a ship's bell and the jingling of small bells on the elves' jackets announced the docking of the Santa Claus ship. The crowd surged to the north side of the pier to greet the jolly figure dressed in red, trimmed with white fur, carrying a large sack and booming a vigorous, "Merry Christmas!" as he ascended the gangway from the dock to the pier.

Verrick looked out into the bay lit with hundreds of small craft circling past the breakwater amidst the sound of carolers singing on the pier and Santa's helpers distributing treats to the ecstatic children. Her toes were cold as she wiggled them in her woolly socks inside her boots, but the warmth of the scene restored her Christmas cheer. She would love to stay longer, but Lionel Parford glanced at his watch and was leading her away from the breakwater, back toward the shore, guiding her through the crowd with his arm at her back, very aware of the shiver that ran through her.

"Cold?"

"No, excited. I've never seen Santa Claus arrive by boat . . ." Her voice trailed off. Never had she seen Santa Claus arrive. Elly didn't want to be seen at some 'noisy kid's event,' where's the fun in that? Her mother preferred a glamorous, sun-filled Caribbean cruise to Christmas with her daughter. *His* mother probably baked Christmas cookies and gathered her family around her.

Verrick sighed deeply, a movement that did not go unnoticed.

Lionel Parford wondered what sad thoughts made her

sigh with such feeling. He reassured her, "We have ten minutes to make it back to Westerly Place by seven o'clock. Don't worry, we'll be on time." He held her hand and walked briskly down the lighted pier. The lights of White Rock twinkled from the hillside as the wind picked up and the first drops of cold rain began to fall.

Verrick switched off her gloomy memories of Christmas past and thought of the evening's performance ahead of her. No one could feel sad with the jolly music of the Christmas pantomime echoing in their ears.

"As you aren't free for dinner this evening, will you join me next Sunday? I've invited my whole family for lunch before the matinee performance of the Christmas pantomime. I've been told it's great fun. Will you come with us?"

They were walking along Marine Drive, Westerly Place was in sight and Verrick was so intent on getting to the theater, slipping into her costume and being on stage on time, she barely registered his invitation.

The blank look of surprise was not the sort of encouragement he had hoped for.

"Have you already seen the pantomime?"

Verrick nodded, swamped by visions of a large happy family sharing lunch and going to the play.

"Then have lunch with us anyway. My mother often asks about you and would be disappointed if you didn't come."

"That's kind of her," Verrick squeaked out, swallowing hard.

They had reached the entrance to Westerly Place. Lionel Parford smiled down at her wind-swept face. "Good. That's settled. Next Sunday at twelve noon. We'll be expecting you."

He held the lobby door open for her. Her eyes darted to her watch—five minutes past seven. She was obviously in a hurry to meet someone else. Lionel Parford didn't detain her. He pressed the elevator button.

To his surprise, she hastily thanked him, then instead of stepping into the elevator, dashed down the stairs to the parking garage.

Regretfully, he watched her scurry away.

Chapter Eight

"No, Mother. I'm not coming to Florida for Christmas."

"Why ever not? You don't plan to stay in that miserable rainy place, do you?"

"Yes, Mother. I'm in a Christmas play until Boxing Day."

"A play? Is there a handsome leading man?"

"No, Mother." If truth be told, the leading man was six feet tall, three hundred pounds, and dressed like a woman. Verrick didn't let her mother in on that fact.

"Then why are you doing it?"

"It's fun, Mother."

"Fun? You call that fun? Why you bury yourself in that dowdy place is beyond me."

"I'm happy here."

"You should be out having a good time. What sort of men can you meet in a Christmas play?"

"I'm not trying to meet men, Mother."

"Well you should be. You're not getting any younger. Why don't you take a trip to Mexico or some place sunny over the holidays? You still have time to book a flight."

Verrick exhaled a weary breath. Her mother would never

understand. She wanted a home of her own, a place to come to not escape from. "I hope you enjoy your cruise, Mother. Are you going alone?"

"Good gracious, no! I met the most wonderful man . . ." Verrick didn't really listen to the rest. She'd heard it so many times before. There was always a "wonderful man" where Elly was concerned. "I'll send you a postcard. Cruises are such fun."

"Merry Christmas, Mother."

Verrick hung up the telephone. She felt restless and irritable. She slipped into her bathing suit and swam twenty vigorous laps before her usual calm self returned. Her mother had a way of leaving her feeling dissatisfied. She never could do anything to gain Elly's approval. She towelled herself off briskly and reminded herself that some things never changed.

It was still early Saturday morning and Verrick had her grocery list in hand, ready to drive to the market. When she turned the key in the ignition of her car, nothing happened. No coughing or sputtering. No lights on the dashboard. Not even a click as she turned the key. Absolutely nothing.

Her car was old but it had never completely failed her like this. Protested, yes, but never down and out refused to start. She slammed the door shut and angrily stomped up the four flights of stairs to her apartment to telephone the garage.

"I'll send a mechanic right over, Miss Grant. Are you sure you didn't leave the lights on?"

"I'm sure."

"Did the motor turn over at all?"

"No, nothing."

"Don't worry, a mechanic should be there within half an hour."

Verrick waited patiently and stoically accepted the verdict.

"It's dead, ma'am. I suspect the whole ignition system needs replacing. We'll have to take it to the shop for a thorough inspection."

"How long will that take?"

"Two . . . three days, maybe longer. A car this old . . . it might take a while to locate parts."

Verrick shrugged defeat. "Do what you can."

"We will, ma'am. I'll phone and let you know what has to be done before we begin." He gave her a fatherly look as he wiped his greasy hands on his overalls. "The repairs may be more expensive than buying a new car."

Verrick grimaced.

He patted the hood of her faithful old car. "We'll do what we can."

The mechanic called a tow truck and she watched the body of her dented vehicle be hooked up and towed away.

The sleek silver Porsche gliding silently into the parking space beside hers did nothing to lift her spirits. Her car never glided silently and she was going to miss its rattling groans and shaky starts.

Lionel Parford caught sight of the tail end of her car being towed out of the parking garage. Verrick stood wistfully staring after it.

"Car troubles?"

She jumped at the unexpected voice, looking like she'd lost her best friend.

He tried again. "Are you stranded without a car?"

"Oh," Verrick regained her voice. "I suppose I am. They'll let me know for how long once they've given it a full inspection."

He put his hand consolingly on her shoulder. "Don't get your hopes up. That car looked in pretty rough shape."

He said it so solemnly, Verrick couldn't help but smile.

"The mechanic said it might be cheaper to buy a new car than fix my old one."

"That's possible. In the meantime, may I offer you a ride?"

Verrick looked at his shiny car, glinting even in the dim light of the underground garage and at her grubby jeans and scuffed sneakers. "Oh, no. I was only going to the grocery store."

"I'd be glad to take you."

She did need groceries and Saturday was her only free day. "O.K." she agreed. "Drop me at the market and I'll take a taxi back."

"Not necessary. I have to buy groceries myself." He held the door open for her. "Hop in."

Verrick sank into the luxurious leather seat and buckled her seatbelt. The car purred into motion and flowed effortlessly out of the parking lot onto the street. The car's interior was heated and smelled vaguely of leather and a woodsy male cologne. Verrick wasn't used to driving to the grocery store in such splendor. Her car gasped and jerked, it's motor making plenty of noise to alert even deaf pedestrians of its approach.

Verrick grinned to herself. Not only were their two cars complete opposites. Here was Lionel Parford immaculately dressed in suit and tie and she in old jeans, a well-worn parka and scruffy sneakers. Funny . . . she didn't feel uncomfortable with him. And he didn't seem the least concerned about her appearance. But she told herself she really should try harder to look professional . . . at least neat and tidy.

Thankfully, the market was only a few miles away and they were already pulling into the parking lot. Verrick searched about in her pockets and found her crumpled shopping list, meeting Lionel Parford's eyes as she clutched it in her gloved hand.

"I forget what I come to buy unless it's written down. When I get home and put things away, I suddenly remember the things I needed but didn't buy." She was babbling on, flustered and unfocused, not at all like her usual self. He had the most gorgeous brown eyes.

With their respective grocery carts, they started off in

opposite directions, Verrick to the produce section and Lionel Parford to the meat department at the far end of the store. Verrick pondered as she selected carrots and put them into a produce bag. I suppose it makes more sense to pick out produce last, then it's on top, not squashed at the bottom of the cart under all the heavy tins and bottles. Trust that man to do it right.

She had a long list and was careful in her choices, reading labels and comparing prices. If she was going to eat it, she figured she deserved to be fussy. Lionel Parford would likely be out of the shop before she had hardly begun. But Verrick refused to be rushed.

He was sitting on a chair just beyond the checkout counter when Verrick finally pushed her cart up to the cashier. He looked perfectly at ease, in spite of the drooling looks he was getting from some of the female clerks. Verrick fumbled in her purse for the exact change, regardless of the people lined up behind her impatiently expecting her to hurry. At last she was done, her grocery cart full and her handsome neighbor gallantly taking it from her hands and pushing it toward the opening doors leading to the parking lot. He didn't seem the least put out at having had to wait.

"I'm sorry to keep you waiting."

"No problem. I had to get my own shopping done."

He cut off any chance for Verrick to thank him further by opening the trunk of his car and loading her groceries in, lining them up beside his own purchases. He whisked her into the passenger seat and was out of the parking lot before she had time to protest.

Westerly Place was in the opposite direction to which they were heading. Before Verrick could voice the question so plainly visible on her expressive face, he answered it.

"I thought we could check on your car before returning home. They should have given it a full going over by now."

She was about to sputter a reply but he smoothly continued, "It's in the garage on Twenty-Fourth isn't it?"

How could he have known that?

He smiled into her curious blue eyes. And like a mind reader, he answered her question. "I read the name on the side of the tow truck."

It was uncanny how the man knew what she was thinking. She'd have to be careful. It could be embarrassing.

Sure enough, the mechanic had diagnosed her car's problem. "It needs a new transmission and a full tune-up."

"How long?"

"Hard to say. Tomorrow's Sunday, can't get parts. That means I won't get started till Monday at the earliest. I'll give you a call Monday, let you know then."

Verrick grudgingly agreed.

Lionel Parford was quicker to see her problem than she was. "Can you provide a courtesy car in the meantime?"

"I'm sorry, sir. It's being used until Monday afternoon. The lady can have it after that."

He suppressed a pleased smile. He ushered Verrick back into his gleaming Porsche. "Allow me to be your chauffeur until then. I'd hate to see a lady stranded, especially in such dark and stormy weather."

Verrick grinned. "It's broad daylight and the sky is clear."

"You never know. A deluge of rain or a fall of snow could happen any minute."

"Thanks for your offer. But I think I can manage without a chauffeur for a few days."

"How about getting to work Monday morning? At least let me drive you that far."

Verrick pressed her lips tightly together. "That might be a problem . . . I suppose I could take the bus."

"To your office in White Rock?"

"No, no. I'm attending a conference in Vancouver . . ."

"That's settled then. My office is in Vancouver. I'll drop you off on my way to work and you can meet me at my office for a ride home."

Verrick was going to protest but he placed two firm fingers over her lips.

"No arguments. Seven-thirty Monday morning. I'll expect you to be ready."

And that was that. He helped her carry her groceries into her apartment and not another word was said about her lack of transportation.

"Yes, Jenna. I'm enjoying it. The cast is like a big family. I feel I've known them forever and the audiences throw themselves into the zany spirit of the pantomime. We have a great time."

"I worry about you, girl."

"Don't fuss, Jenna. I'm fine."

"I don't feel right leaving you alone at Christmas time. I know how you get weepy and sentimental this time of year."

"I'm all grown up. Forget about me. Join Ralph's family and have a good time. The pantomime runs until the twenty-second, then has two performances on Boxing Day. I'll be too busy to even notice you're out of town."

"Promise me you won't watch those Christmas movies that pull the heart strings and leave us both in tears?"

Jenna laughed. "I promise. Besides, it wouldn't be any fun without you."

"What about Elly?"

"She's taking a Caribbean cruise and my father and his latest wife are wrapped up in their new baby. I can't miss what I've never had, Jenna. Those storybook family Christmases have never been part of my life."

Jenna wasn't easily convinced. Verrick was good at hiding her feelings and her friend suspected a loneliness beneath all that festive cheer and Christmas joy being acted out in the playhouse each evening. "What about that neighbor of yours?"

"Lionel Parford?"

"That's the one."

"He's probably having a traditional Christmas, you know, the kind you see in movies, eggnog around the fireplace, glorious Christmas tree, and the whole extended family gathered together to toast each other's health." She had meant to say it in a teasing manner but she couldn't disguise the wistfulness in her voice. It all sounded so . . . wonderful.

"Have you seen him since he fled your apartment?"

"He drove me to the grocery store yesterday."

"And . . . ?"

"And he's giving me a ride into Vancouver tomorrow. My car is in for repairs again."

"Nice of him."

"He is nice, Jenna . . . kind, considerate, thoughtful. . . ."

"In a word . . . perfect."

"Oh, Jenna, I'm beginning to hate that word. I'm so good at playing make-believe and pretending. I wonder if I've just imagined him to be everything I want him to be. I don't know what to do."

"Accept the ride, Verrick. You never know what may come of it. Love strikes when you least expect it."

"Ha! It's more like pity on his part. I'm stranded without a car and he did the gentlemanly thing offering me a ride. I'm sure it was nothing more than that."

"Give him a chance."

"A chance to what? I don't think I'm his type, Jenna. Haven't you seen the society page pictures of him with the likes of Laureen Geddis? He goes for polished, sophisticated women, the very thing that I am not."

Jenna wasn't going to argue but she didn't think the man would look at Verrick the way he did if he wasn't interested. "Well, he hasn't married one of them, has he? Perhaps he's bored with society women. What about opposites attracting?"

Verrick was quiet for a long pause. "Not these two opposites. We'd be more likely to come to blows."

"That shows there's passion in the works. It wouldn't be boring."

"You're right, Jenna. There's nothing boring about Lionel Parford. But there's no chance of any special relationship between us, either."

"Well, girl, as Elly would say, it's time to get out there shopping for shoes."

"Since when did either of us take advise from my mother?"

"That's true, Verrick. Just promise me you won't sit home and feel sorry for yourself over Christmas. I can't help worrying about you."

"There's nothing to worry about. Bob Harris has convinced me to join his team of flying doctors to visit some remote northern villages between Boxing Day and New Year's Eve. It will be my third trip with the team. I always come back feeling grateful for my blessings. Compared to some of those tough, isolated, rain-drenched mining towns, White Rock is paradise."

"You're a treasure, Verrick. You could be out partying but instead, you're sloshing through snowbanks to poke around in people's mouths. I never could understand your fascination with teeth."

Verrick switched on her tooth fairy voice. "Jenna, dear, life would be miserable without teeth."

"OK. You've got me there. Take care, Verrick." Jenna paused, then added as an afterthought, "Verrick . . . talk to the guy. I know how you clam up when things get personal. Girl, you could go to the moon and never mention it to anyone. Talk about yourself."

"I'm a dentist, Jenna. No one wants to hear 'dentist talk.' " Look how squeamish you get when I mention drilling, root canals and bleeding gums."

"O.K. . . . maybe not dentist stuff . . . but you never talk about yourself."

"That's boring."

"It may not be . . . to the right guy."

"I'll think about it, Jenna."

"That's a good start. I'll call you when we get back from Kelowna."

"Merry Christmas, Jenna. Have fun."

"Mrs. Ross, when Dr. Grant arrives let me know right away."

"Even if you're in conference?"

"Yes, Mrs. Ross. This is important. I'll cut the conference short the instant Dr. Grant arrives."

"Yes, sir."

Mrs. Ross continued on with her typing as the team of architects conferred on the proposed convention center drawings in Mr. Parford's office. She was curious about this Dr. Grant. It was seldom her boss demanded someone be given such preferential treatment. As she typed up the letter he'd dictated that morning, she wondered if Mr. Parford was suffering from some illness, something serious enough to have a doctor make a private visit.

After thinking about it, her boss had been acting strangely this last while. He spent an enormous amount of time alone in his office over his drawing board. He was working on some project she didn't know about. That was unusual.

Then there was that incident with Miss Geddis. Mr. Parford wasn't usually brusque with her, but he'd refused to take her out to lunch.

But he didn't look in poor health. He was more quiet and brooding than usual, as though something were troubling him, but he was still vibrant, energetic and the most handsome man she'd ever set eyes on.

He seemed happy and excited about Dr. Grant's arrival, not worried as he would be if the doctor was bringing bad news. Mrs. Ross focused on her computer screen and continued on with the day's correspondence. It was puzzling.

An attractive young woman came quietly into the office. She was dressed for the cold day, unwrapping a woolly blue scarf from around her neck and pulling off matching gloves. She wore a soft gray coat and smiled at Mrs. Ross with such warm friendliness, the secretary stopped halfway through a sentence, looked up, and smiled back. The woman had gorgeous blue eyes and the most gentle voice.

"Don't let me disturb your work. I'm a bit early, I can wait."

"Is Mr. Parford expecting you?"

"He is."

The sunshine radiance of Verrick's smile warmed Mrs. Ross through. She'd buzz her boss, regardless of the conference he was in. This pleasant young lady deserved his attention.

Verrick saw the secretary reaching toward the intercom. "No, don't interrupt his work. He is in a meeting, isn't he?"

"Yes, but I should let him know you're here."

"Oh no. I can wait. I hate being interrupted halfway through a job, don't you?"

Mrs. Ross agreed. This thoughtful woman was the opposite of that brassy Miss Geddis. She was admiring the sketches of finished projects that adorned the walls, graceful in her movements and enthusiastic in her praise. "I like this one, how clever, fitting it into the rock outcropping like that. Do you have a favorite?"

The usually reserved Mrs. Ross happily got up from behind her desk and pointed out the sea front mansion with sweeping decks and magnificent views.

"That is grand, isn't it? Mr. Parford is talented. I don't think I could live with the ocean lapping at my window ledge, though. I'd probably be seasick every time the wind came up." Mrs. Ross chuckled. Such a delightful young lady, no uppity airs about her. The two women continued down the length of the wall discussing Mr. Parford's talent as an architect. Neither one noticed his office door open, or the gentlemen starting to leave as the meeting broke up.

Lionel Parford was alerted that something was out of the

ordinary when he heard his secretary actually laughing. That only happened on rare occasions. With lifted eyebrows, his wary eyes scanned the outer office and settled on the shapely figure in the soft gray coat.

Forgetting his fellow architects now filing into the hallway, he crossed the length of the office in four giant strides and stood beside Verrick, his hand at her back, before she realized his meeting had ended. Her smile stopped him in his tracks, melting the harsh look he was aiming at Mrs. Ross and the angry words of reprimand for not announcing Verrick when she arrived. A stillness hushed the three people as they stood in front of the display wall of architectural drawings. Mrs. Ross cringed, expecting a blast of criticism for not obeying her boss' orders to the letter. But the blast never came.

Lionel Parford looked down into those blue eyes and forgot everything. To his secretary's amazement, the corners of his mouth lifted and he smiled a full, welcoming smile, the likes of which she'd never seen on that handsome face before. The silence seemed to last for ages, but it was actually only a few seconds.

"Have you been waiting long?"

"Oh no. Your secretary was kind enough to show me these drawings. You're very clever. I like your work."

Mrs. Ross was grateful for the words of praise. She seized her opportunity and hastened back to her desk before Mr. Parford could tear his gaze from those gentle blue eyes and blast her with his anger.

This must be the Dr. Grant he was expecting . . . interesting. The way Mr. Parford was hypnotized by her lovely smile and soothing voice, she could operate on him without anesthetic and he'd never notice. Her sweet-tempered manner must put her most nervous patients at ease.

Lionel Parford jolted back into the present at the sound of Mrs. Ross' typing. Verrick was smiling at him with that dazzling look she had, and he quite forgot everything he planned to say to her. He remembered now that she said she liked his work. "Would you like to see my latest project?"

He guided Verrick into his inner office and directed her to his drafting table. All the sketches and floor plans were laid out on view as well as detailed plans for the exterior finishing.

Verrick studied all the intricate blueprints, nodded occasionally, and bent over the table more closely to inspect some fine point on the drawings.

Lionel watched her every move, holding his breath, eager to hear her opinion. Much to his surprise, her approval meant a great deal to him. He was not disappointed.

She turned to him with a radiant smile. "It's perfect. The most wonderful home I could imagine. It has everything just right, like in a story book. I thought such a thing only existed in dreams." She turned and admired the plans once more. Lionel moved to stand behind her, an incredible lightness in his step. Her praise meant more than all the architectural awards in creation.

Verrick's eyes clouded over and her happy face turned somber. She looked up soulfully into Lionel Parford's brown eyes. "It must be difficult to design a magnificent house like this and then hand it over to your client." She scanned his face for traces of sadness. "Aren't you tempted to break into the house after the new owners have moved in, to sit in the armchair by the fire, admire the view at sunset, or cook a meal in the kitchen, just to see how it feels, to be sure everything came out exactly right?"

He was touched by her concern for his feelings at handing over one of his creations to its owners. He'd never felt the desire to move into any of the homes he'd designed. None were exactly right for his own tastes, that is, not until he designed the one presently spread out on his drawing table. Verrick's possessive attitude toward this house pleased him but he didn't let on by either word or expression. He maintained his perfectly controlled demeanor and made the quiet understatement, "I'm glad you like it."

"Like it? I love it! It's exactly how a home should be. All those years living in a stark room at boarding school, I conjured up a house like this in my mind, imagining what it would be like to live in a real home, a garden to play in, space for everyone, and a feeling of warmth and welcome at the mere sight of the place."

She pointed to a spot to one side of the kitchen. "What is this set of rooms for?"

Lionel bent over her, his tangy aftershave lotion wafting past her nostrils. "That's the caretaker's suite. A house this size will require staff, a live-in housekeeper and gardener at least. And they deserve accommodations of their own."

Verrick clapped her hands together. "You think of everything. I never considered that." She beamed up at him with such joy and enthusiasm. They had the same taste in houses and that realization pleased him more than he could express. She had sounded so wistful when she talked about the home of her dreams.

The desire to hold her in his arms and kiss away the sadness in her voice was strong, but he kept his distance. He must wait, she didn't seem aware of his feelings for her. She needed time and he would give it to her. But, oh how he'd like to build that home of her dreams for her!

"This house is presently under construction. Would you like to visit the building site? It can easily be arranged."

Her face brightened. She was so transparent. "Could I? I'd love that." She thought for a moment. "It's in the country, right?"

He nodded.

"Perfect." She grinned. "I knew it would be."

The spicy fragrance of cinnamon, cloves and ginger permeated Verrick's kitchen as she pulled the last tray of gingerbread men from the oven. She was up early mixing dough, rolling it evenly, and cutting out shapes. She watched closely as they baked. She didn't want burnt fingers and toes on her gingerbread men.

Now she was stirring the icing to decorate them. It helped to keep busy. She was nervous and excited about meeting the whole Parford family. Those members she had met were friendly and welcoming.

She piped white icing around the outlines of the smiling men lined up on her kitchen counter. Gingerbread was her favorite, she hoped the Parford family liked it, too. She couldn't turn up for lunch empty-handed.

It was kind of Lionel Parford to invite her; she had to be gracious and accept, try as she might to wriggle out. He insisted. So she nervously flitted about her kitchen carefully preparing the most delectable gift basket of gingerbread men. She tied the big red bow and stood back to admire. Her eye caught the clock on her microwave and she flew to the bedroom to change, comb her hair and apply a touch of makeup. Her cheeks were flushed from the heat of the oven and her eyes sparkled with excitement. She was happy and frightened all at the same time. She was afraid she'd dreamed about families for so long, the real thing couldn't possibly measure up.

The remembrances of being awkward and in-the-way during Elly's flirtatious parties haunted her. But she wasn't given time to dwell on unsettling thoughts. A loud knock on her door set her in motion.

Gavin Parford's friendly face greeted her. "Lion sent me to fetch you." He leaned closer to whisper, "I think he was afraid you'd back out at the last minute."

Verrick laughed. Gavin would never know how close to the truth that was. "I'm ready," she said, less confidently than she intended.

Gavin whistled at the basket of gingerbread men. "Great! Everyone loves gingerbread but my mother's cook refuses to cut shapes we gobble down in less time than they take to make. 'Works of art are meant to be admired, not swallowed down in the blink of any eye,' she says."

Verrick appreciated Gavin's easy chatter as they walked the short distance to the other penthouse apartment on the fourth floor. She felt stage fright, worse than anything she'd ever felt in the playhouse.

A splendid wreath, fragrant with fresh cedar and pine, adorned the door. Gavin escorted her into a room filled with people, cheerful voices and childish laughter. Light flooded the apartment but still a beautiful Christmas tree was lit, casting rainbows of light into the festive group. Verrick inhaled, taking in all the decorations and happy people. It really was like a page from a storybook. It was more than she had ever dreamed of.

Gavin swept her across the living room floor to where his mother was seated with a blond-headed grandson on her knee.

"You've met my mother?"

Verrick smiled, the butterflies in her stomach settling as the older woman stood and kissed her cheek. "How lovely to see you again, dear. I'm glad you could join us." She gestured to the little boy on the sofa. "This is Jason. He's never been to a play before and hopes it won't be scary. Lion tells us you've already seen it, perhaps you could give the children some idea what to expect."

"Not only have I seen it, I actually have a small role in the Christmas play." She didn't give anyone time to react to that information.

Verrick sat down on a low footstool and briefly told the pantomime fairy tale. "But you mustn't be frightened. There is a Christmas fairy who looks after the hero. Whenever the evil King Rat is up to his nasty deeds, you have only to call for the fairy and she'll come to the rescue."

It wasn't only the children who were enchanted by her soft, musical voice. Her host stood behind her admiring the way she entered a child's world of imagination with no selfish thoughts about appearing silly. She had a wonderful way with children. But the tender look and brilliant smile aimed at Verrick was more about that little fact she'd dropped. She had a part in the pantomime—that's where she'd been every evening. He was delighted to hear it.

Rachel noticed his rapt attention and winked at her twin brother. She was near her due date but felt in marvelous health, as excited to attend the Christmas play as the smallest of the children.

When Verrick stood up to walk over to Rachel, it was not Gavin beside her but Lion. She shivered at the touch of his hand gently helping her to her feet. It wasn't like her to be bashful, but she blushed. He took her by surprise, she hadn't expected him to be so close.

He was dressed casually in a deep burgundy sweater over a white shirt and dark tie. But it was the soft brown of his eyes that captured Verrick's attention. And he was smiling.

"Welcome. You're a gifted storyteller. Thank you for putting the children's fears to rest."

She stared at him dumbly, for what seemed ages. Verrick cleared her throat but no words came to her rescue.

Lionel Parford seemed not to notice. He took her arm and guided her to the group of people by the punch bowl. "Let me introduce you to the rest of my family."

Patiently, he introduced each of his relatives. Verrick had recovered her voice and soon felt among friends. Each person greeted her with familiarity, as though they had all met her many times before. Lionel Parford didn't leave her side. It pleased him the way his family reacted to Verrick Grant but no hint of that pleasure showed on his unruffled features.

Lunch was set out buffet style with a wonderful selection of hot dishes, salads, sliced meats, breads and pickles—a selection of favorites, judging by the way the children filled their plates and ate with ravenous appetites. Verrick was swept into the cheerful conversation and gentle teasing, passing dishes and assisting children, very aware of being in the midst of a close-knit family and loving every minute of it.

Although he was host, Mr. Perfect was at ease, making sure everyone had all they needed but not fussing or making anyone uncomfortable. It ran smoothly, festive and delicious, spectacular without any apparent stress or bother, as perfect as the host himself.

Verrick glanced at her watch. It was time to make a mad dash to the theater and whip into her costume and makeup. But she hated to tear herself away from this family. It filled her heart with gladness. Fairy Snowflake was going to be a bit disheveled this Sunday matinee, but Verrick didn't care. She was living in a cherished dream and didn't want to wake up.

Sonya Parford broke the spell, suggesting the children use the bathroom and begin getting ready. The play was to begin at two o'clock and they didn't want to be late. The adults made quick work of clearing the table, putting food away and filling the dishwasher. Verrick watched starry-eyed. For so many years, she alone, had cleared the table, washed the dishes and set the kitchen to rights. Elly frowned upon "work meant for servants." But the Parford family seemed to enjoy working together, sharing the chores.

Verrick absolutely must make a break for it now—the pantomime couldn't start without her. She was first on stage.

Lionel Parford noticed the anxious look she cast toward the door as the last of the dishes was stacked in the dishwasher. "Forgive me. I quite forgot you must be anxious to get to the theater to be ready before the rest of us arrive. Can I drive you there?"

Time was slipping away on her and she had to dash but the tender note in his voice and the way his arm rested so comfortably around her waist made leaving difficult. She pulled her wits together long enough to answer his question.

She gazed up into those dark brown eyes, "Oh, no. You come later and bring your family. It's quicker if I drive myself." Her voice was husky. There was so much more to be said between them, but precious minutes were ticking away and she had to run.

She bid a quick farewell to Mrs. Parford and all the gathered family members, slipping on her coat, then saying, "I hope you enjoy the pantomime. Merry Christmas."

Amid returned wishes of 'Merry Christmas,' Verrick ran to the elevator and thankfully, her rental car started on the first turn of the key in the ignition.

White Rock Playhouse was bustling with people. Christmas carols played from speakers and happy excitement filled the air as people produced their tickets, received programs and were shown to their seats. The Parford family filled three full rows near the front, Rachel being seated on the aisle, "just in case," her older brother informed her.

At last the lights were dimmed, the final stragglers took their seats, voices were shushed and the musical introduction began. A blast of smoke from stage left, and the Christmas fairy appeared. Her hair was loose, sprinkled with silver dust and her sparkling gown glittered in the spotlights.

A collective "ooh" greeted her appearance, a real-live fairy stepped out of a fairy tale. Instantly the tone of make-believe was set, and the audience was carried along by this magical vision. Her voice was low, as if sharing secrets. Lionel Parford smiled at his nieces and nephews leaning forward, unwilling to miss a single word. Fairy Snowflake told the audience they must believe for the magic to work. And when she asked, "Do you believe in fairies?" the response was an overwhelming, "Yes!"

She disappeared from the stage. The curtain opened and the brightly costumed chorus began its rollicking opening number.

Sonya Parford glanced at her eldest son as the happy tale

unfolded. For a serious man who enjoyed the opera and ballet, this was a light-hearted diversion, but he seemed as enchanted as little Jason who had wriggled onto Lion's knee in order to see better.

The smile on his face had more to do with his discovery of where Verrick had been every evening this past month than with the slapstick antics and silly songs on stage.

So this is why she's been refusing my invitations and dashing off in that old car of hers every night? She isn't spending every waking hour with the driver of the Mercedes. She hasn't been in the arms of a lover or partying till all hours of the night. She's been delighting audiences with the Christmas pantomime. And he, too, was delighted. Although not exactly for the same reason as every other member of the audience.

During the intermission, chattering crowds thronged the lobby, but one tall blond man was off in the farthest corner talking on his cell phone.

"That's right. Immediately. To the White Rock Playhouse."

Someone at the other end must have been putting up an argument, but his voice was insistent. "I don't care what it costs. Yes, two dozen."

With satisfaction, he snapped the phone into its case and returned it to his pocket.

Everyone was eagerly settling into their seats when he slipped in beside his nephew.

Sonya Parford leaned over and smiled. "Lion, why didn't you tell us Verrick was in the pantomime? The girl is priceless. She captures your heart the instant she steps on the stage."

"I didn't know, Mother. Fairy Snowflake is good at keeping secrets."

Jason resettled himself on his uncle's lap and giggled. "Fairies have to keep secrets, Uncle Lion."

It seemed so simple to a child. But Lionel Parford couldn't help wondering why Verrick Grant didn't mention her role in the Christmas play to him earlier. Then he remembered she was late and rushing off when he had invited her. Perhaps she hadn't been keeping secrets, just run off her feet trying to keep up with all her commitments. Come to think of it, she said very little about herself. He only discovered she was a dentist because of a throbbing tooth.

When the final rousing chorus of "We Wish You a Merry Christmas" was sung and the entire cast took its third bow, an usher presented a startled Fairy Snowflake with a giant florist-wrapped bouquet of two dozen long-stemmed red roses. Her blurry eyes looked out over the footlights, unseeing, but instinctively knowing who the donor was. She mouthed the words, "Thank you," untied the ribbon and flitted about onstage distributing red roses to each of the cast members, as light and delicate as the fairy she was pretending to be.

The audience clapped and cheered until finally the curtain closed for the last time.

"That was delightful," Sonya Parford commented, helping her grandson on with his coat. "Be sure to tell Verrick how much we enjoyed it. Such a generous thing to do over Christmas, giving pleasure to so many people."

The large Parford family scattered to their cars, heading to their respective homes.

Lionel Parford returned to Westerly Place, slipping his Porsche neatly into his parking spot, noting the empty space beside his own.

His neighbor was definitely full of surprises.

She's a master at make-believe but what is the real Verrick Grant like behind the roles she plays?

He took the stairs two at a time, determined to find the answer to that interesting question.

Chapter Nine

V errick drove straight from the theater to the office Christmas party, secretly wishing all these festivities could be spread out over the entire year, not jammed into a few hectic weeks in December. She had no time to think about the lovely family gathering the Parfords had allowed her to share, she toasted the season with her fellow dentists, the office staff and their husbands and wives. It wasn't until late Sunday night when she slipped into her frosty car, warming it up to drive home that she noticed the long-stemmed red rose on the passenger seat where she'd placed it after dashing from the theater.

She picked it up and inhaled, the sweet fragrance teasing her nostrils as the car's heater began to warm the chilly space. She sighed. A summer rose on this cold winter night—what a beautiful thing. Only Lionel Parford would come up with such a thoughtful gesture. She put it gently down on the seat, started her protesting car and drove through streets turning icy in the freezing temperature, warmed by the gift of a red rose.

She was exhausted, sleepy and in a state of dreaminess. Her mind was drifting—a loving family, a cozy fire, and Lion. She loved him. He hadn't made fun of her having a role in the Christmas pantomime . . . in fact, he seemed very pleased about it.

The wail of a siren and the flashing lights of a speeding ambulance jolted her back to reality. She couldn't love Mr. Perfect. With her short-sighted clumsiness and make-believe fantasies, she only imagined it. But it felt real. No, she couldn't love him. She was caught up in Christmas fantasies.

She gave herself a very sensible lecture as she drove slowly and carefully home over slippery streets. But when she carried that red rose into her bedroom, placed it in a bud vase, and set it beside her bed, all those sensible warnings vanished. She loved him. It would be her secret. But she couldn't deny it, no matter how hard she tried.

"Dr. Grant, there's a delivery for you."

Verrick straightened from an inspection of her elderly patient's mouth. "Thank you, Mary. Hold it until I'm free."

She smiled reassuringly at the frail woman in the dentist chair. "You're doing a fine job, Mrs. Whitby. There are no new cavities and your receding gums have stayed the same." She patted the veined hand still gripping the arm of the chair tightly. "You have nothing to worry about." The deep grooves around the pale eyes softened and Mrs. Whitby lifted her gray head as Verrick helped her to a sitting position.

"I was so worried, Dr. Grant."

Verrick's friendly smile and unhurried manner put the tense woman at ease. "It's not uncommon for teeth to be sensitive to hot and cold. Just continue with the special toothpaste and I'm sure you'll have no more troubles."

Mrs. Whitby's relieved smile was Karen's signal to remove the bib and assist the patient to the lobby. She returned a few minutes later with a beautiful bouquet of daffodils and hyacinths in a pottery vase.

"The receptionists are speculating. Who's it from?"

Verrick opened the little card and read:

Thank you, Verrick, for your delightful performance.
It was like a breath of springtime on a cold winter's
day.

Sonya Parford

"So . . . who is it from?"

"A pantomime fan."

A groan of disappointment was faintly audible over the
open intercom.

Karen relayed the news. "Sorry, Mary. It wasn't from
him."

Verrick raised her eyebrows. "Him?"

"You know . . ." Karen stammered, "The difficult patient
. . . the one whose tooth you filled before he knew what
was happening."

"Mr. Parford?"

"That's the one."

"Why would he send me flowers?"

Karen looked down at her hands. "We thought you'd
touched a nerve, so to speak. You have to admit, the man
had . . . a reaction."

Verrick laughed. "I touched a nerve all right. The man
thinks I'm crazed. Tell the office staff to stop taking bets
on Mr. Parford. This is a dentist office not a match-
maker's."

Karen giggled. "We can always hope."

Verrick placed the lovely bouquet atop a bookcase so
everyone could enjoy the flowers. "Send down our next
patient, Mary."

She may not have revealed it to her assistant, but Verrick
was touched by the kind gesture.

Lionel Parford had carefully read the pantomime pro-
gram and noted there was no performance on Mondays. He
was pleased when he saw Verrick's car in its parking spot
as he pulled in beside it. She was home this evening. He
had an invitation to deliver and he wanted to do it in per-

son, not to some answering machine which was all he ever got when he dialed her number.

But he was to be disappointed.

When he knocked on her door after dinner, there was no answer. He stomped back to his own suite and closed the door with enough force to rattle the dishes on the shelves. *Drat that woman! Does she never stay home?*

Verrick was in Vancouver, making final plans with a group of doctors to fly into a remote region on December twenty-seventh. The four-day trip was planned to the smallest detail.

"You've flown with us before, Dr. Grant. Remember to be prepared for deep snow and frigid conditions. Bring a good sleeping bag, waterproof clothes, lined boots, and lots of dry woolly socks."

Verrick nodded. She had her backpack and hiking supplies ready.

"We're taking a full week's supply of freeze-dried food. There's no guarantee the local residents will be feeding us or providing shelter. We have a camp stove and tents to accommodate us all, if worse comes to worse."

"How about examination rooms, assistants, dental equipment?"

"We have use of the first aid room at the mining camp and the community centers in two of the villages. It's primitive, but we make do. Our basic aim is prevention before any condition gets too serious. These patients have no access to regular dental care and their medical plans don't cover it."

Dr. Harris motioned toward Verrick. "Dr. Grant will confirm how grateful these people are to have their teeth taken care of. Some have been in pain for months."

"Are there no local dentists?"

"No closer than a two-day journey."

The young doctor joining the team for the first time,

looked at Verrick's slender figure and wondered aloud, "How do you get those tough loggers, miners and back-woods characters into a dentist chair?"

Dr. Harris laughed. "Wait until you see her in action. She's better than a night at the movies."

The young man looked incredulous. "This I've got to see!"

The four doctors agreed on a departure time and made a final check of their supplies list.

"I'm driving in from Langley that morning, Verrick. I can pick you up. It will save leaving two cars freezing up on the airport lot."

"Thanks, I'd appreciate that. You've seen my car. It doesn't take kindly to being left out in the weather for days."

"A church group in the valley has donated toothbrushes and dental floss, so you'll have plenty to distribute. Several of the Indian children have been asking when the tooth fairy will come back."

Verrick grinned.

"Rest up. You're in for a demanding four days."

"I'll be ready."

Dr. Harris thumped her on the back. "Good girl. We can always count on you."

It wasn't until Thursday, two days before Christmas, that Lionel Parford finally got the opportunity to deliver his invitation.

Verrick's dental office was closed until after the New Year, the pantomime only had two more performances, both on Boxing Day, and Verrick was taking the time to check over all her hiking equipment and camping supplies. Her backpack was laid out and all her gear spread over her bedroom floor when she was interrupted by a knock on her door.

In spite of the stern lecture she had given herself, and

her determination to keep her feelings for Lionel Parford a secret, Verrick's face lit with a beaming smile when she saw who was at her door.

He wasn't doing much better himself.

Neither spoke, merely drank in the sight of each other. Then Verrick blushed and said in a quiet voice, "Thank you for the beautiful roses." She was going to say more but he was looking at her with such an unusual expression, the words stuck in her throat. "Would you like to come in?"

His face relaxed into a warm smile then, and he followed her into her living room, the peachy-orange color of the walls in sharp contrast to the bank of gray fog stretching out across Semiahmoo Bay.

Verrick was jittery and restlessly shifted her weight from one foot to the other before settling into an armchair. Lionel Parford had an unnerving habit of staring her down, waiting for her to give him her attention. That wasn't hard. He was all she thought about most of the time. She looked down at her hands. She didn't want him to see the adoring look she couldn't disguise.

He took it all in with a gentle smile.

He was truly handsome when he smiled like that. All the lines on his face softened and those deep brown eyes looked as delicious as hot fudge syrup.

"My whole family enjoyed the pantomime, even Father with his scholarly English Literature background." He pinned her with those probing dark eyes. "Why didn't you mention that you had a part in the play?"

Verrick clasped her hands in her lap and swallowed. She heard her mother's voice berating her, calling her childish, and making fun of her play-acting. How could she tell this man why she wasn't in the habit of talking about her make-believe world?

The woeful look on her face must have spoken for her.

"Were you afraid people would think less of Dr. Grant if they knew she had a secret life?"

"Not really. My friends know I'm great at pretending . . . I just don't talk about it much. It sounds crazy, but make-believe is my way of keeping sane."

"Not crazy at all. But your performance is something to brag about. I admire your talent and generosity, my whole family does. Your role in the Christmas pantomime gives great pleasure to so many."

Verrick took a deep breath. He wasn't finished yet.

"Fairy Snowflake touched the hearts of everyone, adult and child alike." He paused long enough to let that sink in then continued to take her breath away. "My mother asked me to invite you for Christmas Day." He didn't give her the chance to refuse. "I know you've been run off your feet working by day and performing by night, but we'd be honored to have you celebrate Christmas with us."

Verrick's first impulse was to say, "No." She didn't want to be pitied, to be taken in like some orphan.

But there was no pity on Lion's face. "It would be like catching a leprechaun having the Christmas fairy in our midst. Rachel said it would surely bring us all luck. Please come, Verrick."

"It's a family time. I don't want to intrude."

He laughed. "No one could be more welcome."

He sounded sincere. "Then . . . yes. I'd love to come."

For a man who usually appeared so confident, Lionel Parford relaxed, as if he'd been tensed for a refusal. "Good. I'll pick you up in the morning so you can attend church with the family. We have dinner at midday. It was a custom that began when we were small children so the excitement of the day was dealt with early and we could settle down to sleep by bedtime." He grinned. "We're grown now. But the custom persists."

Verrick envied traditions. Her family had none. Elly didn't want to be tied down by bothersome rules. She wanted to have fun and a traditional Christmas was no part of that.

Verrick smiled wistfully. "Thank your mother for her invitation."

He reached out and took her hand. "The invitation was not only from my mother." He pinned her with those warm brown eyes. "The invitation was from me, as well." He bend his head and kissed her hand. He could feel her trembling.

Verrick just stared at him, all her love and longing in her eyes, if she had but known it.

Lionel Parford wanted to more than kiss her hand but he reluctantly got to his feet and turned to leave. "Until Saturday, then." His voice was warm and enchanting as if making promises of good things to come.

Verrick repeated, "Until Saturday," trying to conceal her racing pulse and shortness of breath. She wanted to jump up and down with joy but she calmly mimicked his proper manners.

She escorted him to the door, and closed it softly behind him.

Only then did she jump up and down and glow with anticipation. She wasn't going to be spending Christmas Day alone. She would get to share it with a real family. And Lionel would be there, too.

She left the sorting of sweaters, thermal underwear, and wool socks for later. She knew exactly which gift to get for Mrs. Parford—that vase she'd admired in the antique shop, and perhaps, a sinfully expensive box of Callebaut chocolates, as well. But what could she give to Lionel Parford?

Maybe she couldn't give anything from herself . . . but perhaps a gift from the tooth fairy. She thought about it as she threaded her way through crowds of shoppers. She would be hiding behind her make-believe guise, but the tooth fairy could give him a gift without revealing Verrick's feelings.

*   *   *

Standing in the church with Lionel Parford's solid strength beside her on one side and his gentle caring mother on the other, Verrick could be forgiven if she let her thoughts wander. The organ reverberated through the small stone chapel and Verrick shivered with delight. Even if just for this one day, she felt her dreams were fulfilled. Voices raised in a joyful hymn echoed the happiness bubbling inside her. This was the Christmas she imagined when the other girls had gone home for the holidays and she was left behind at boarding school.

The day unfolded just as she hoped it would. The large dining room table had space for every member of the family and together, they relished the fine roast goose, the assortment of vegetables, breads, and side dishes. The joy of being welcomed so warmly touched Verrick deeply, so much so she felt almost weepy. And although she delighted in the sumptuous feast, she ate very little.

Seated across from her, Lionel Parford noticed her helping Jason cut his meat and butter his roll. The little boy had attached himself to her, convinced she was a Christmas miracle with the power to vanish if he didn't stay close. He also noticed her lack of appetite.

Perhaps this crowd of noisy relatives was overwhelming to a woman used to her solitude. But she joined in the conversation so easily. He knew his family liked her. It was important to him that she felt comfortable with the people he loved.

Verrick only nibbled the piece of mince pie set before her. Her stomach was doing somersaults. She was as excited as any small child at Christmas. She couldn't help it, even if Lionel glared at her as if to tell her she must clean her plate. Her appetite was gone and she couldn't force down any more food.

After everyone had eaten their fill, heaping praise upon Birgit and Mrs. Parford for outdoing themselves this year, they settled in the living room, before a blazing fire. The large spruce tree was decorated with family treasures, many of them hand-made by the Parford children over the years. Verrick felt a tightness in her throat, loving the way each child's contribution was valued. How unlike Elly's disdainful voice saying, "How primitive! Throw it out. No one wants amateur attempts at art cluttering the house." Verrick had been crushed. She'd worked so hard to make that clay ornament to please her mother.

Mr. Parford, with his scholarly manner, handed out the gaily-wrapped gifts from under the tree. With squeals of delight and hoots of laughter, packages were opened and gifts admired.

"Verrick, this is lovely. Thank you. It's the very thing I'd have bought for myself." Sonya Parford's genuine pleasure thrilled Verrick. She'd never given her mother a gift that hadn't been criticized—too bright, too dull, too large, too small, not my taste, not in fashion—all those hurtful phrases that wounded her.

With twinkling eyes, Mr. Parford put a long thin package in Verrick's hands. The card read:

Merry Christmas Verrick
  May your prince always be charming
  Gavin

She unwrapped a poster, in full living color of the Halloween party when the tooth fairy danced with Prince Charming. She held it up for everyone to see, and laughed.

"Oh no!" Lionel Parford groaned. "Am I never going to get the chance to live that down?"

His brothers and sisters answered as one, "Never!"

He assumed a look of agony, but the laughter in his eyes betrayed the truth.

Next she opened a small box from Mrs. Parford. It contained a little china figurine, antique, but still the gown and features of the girl were unblemished. Verrick crossed over

to where Mrs. Parford was seated and kissed her elderly
cheek. "Thank you," she whispered. "I've never owned
anything so delicate. I'm short-sighted and tend to drop
things. No one dared risk valuable porcelain near me."

Sonya Parford held her trembling hand. "I thought the
girl resembled you, dear, with her blue eyes and wavy
hair." She saw tears welling up in Verrick's eyes and said
nothing more to distress her. It was as though the dear child
had never before received a Christmas gift.

In spite of the noise, giggles, and outpourings of thanks,
Lionel Parford was aware that Verrick Grant was very
quiet, and her big blue eyes were swimming. The sparkling
silver package in his hands could be from no one else. It
was outrageously festive, laughing up at him, daring him
to open it. He met Verrick's eyes across the room and untied the glittering ribbon. Inside he found a jewelry box, in
which sat a finely-made silver keyring sitting on a bed of
cotton. When he picked it up, the three enamel teeth hanging from it tinkled together. One tooth was entirely white
enamel, one was filled with silver, and the third was etched
with jagged red shafts depicting pain.

Rachel laughed at the sight of it. "Lion, how fitting! Your
worst nightmare. A constant reminder to visit your dentist."

"It is, indeed." He grimaced at the three teeth. "Some
things I don't need to be reminded about."

Rachel could agree with that. The way Lion kept gazing
at Verrick, visiting her was not something he needed to be
prodded to do. But she wasn't going to say that out loud.
Some things her big brother had to figure out for himself.

A final gift was set before Verrick. The card was signed
with Lionel's sprawling hand. Verrick carefully unfastened
the strips of tape and withdrew a breathtaking landscape
painting, framed in a similar manner to the ones hanging
in her living room. On first glance, it was a forest scene,
rich shades of green with golden shafts of sunlight. But on
closer inspection, beneath the ferns and wildflowers on the

forest floor, were elves, sprites and fairies. They were skill-
fully concealed, only glimpses and brief snatches teased the
eye.

Verrick loved it. He understood. She found it hard to lift
her head and meet Lionel's eyes as he watched her from
across the room. Instead of the happy smile and the kiss
his mother was rewarded with, he looked into soulful blue
eyes on the verge of tears. She was struggling to form
words to thank him but it was all too much.

Reading the signs, Lionel Parford swept across the room,
sheltering Verrick from any curious glances that may be
cast her way. "You need a break from all this hubbub.
Come and tour my mother's greenhouse. It's her pride and
joy." Before she could answer, his arm was helping her to
her feet and guiding her toward the kitchen. He said not a
word, merely ushered her out through the kitchen door into
the heated greenhouse. The humid air smelled of greenery
and damp potting soil. He gently sat beside her on a bench
facing a jungle of hot-house plants, and turned questioning
eyes on her downcast head.

"Care to talk about it?"

Verrick swallowed. Her voice was barely above a whisper. "I've never spent Christmas with a family."

He didn't say anything critical or belittling, just stretched
his arm along the back of the garden seat and held her close
against his chest.

It was warm and comforting Verrick snuggled closer. He
was so solid and smelled so wonderful. She could happily
stay here beside him forever.

She now knew a happy family holiday could be real, not
just her imagination. She sniffled, thinking of all those
years she'd believed it never could be.

He placed a crisp linen handkerchief in her hand and
stroked her back as she quietly let her tears escape.

Verrick was embarrassed, getting weepy on a day filled
with good cheer. "I'm sorry . . ." she began.

He kissed her forehead, then said quietly close against her ear, "Don't be sorry."

Verrick tried again. "Thank you for the painting. It's magic. I'll hang it where I can see it every day."

"Was that what made you cry?"

"No, no. It was everything all put together—your family's kindness, the spirit of Christmas, and gifts—I couldn't hold back the tears. I often get weepy this time of year— not sadness, exactly. I'm just overwhelmed by it all.

This was the most she'd revealed about herself to anyone, except Jenna.

"I gather Elly didn't enjoy motherhood, home, and family holidays."

"No . . . she likes parties, though."

He could imagine. Not much of a life for a girl growing up.

Verrick took a deep breath and wiped her eyes. "I'm not usually tearful. I don't know what's gotten into me."

She didn't see his gentle smile. "No need to apologize."

Her head rested on his shoulder. She wasn't quite ready to meet his eyes. His body warmth was comforting and the masculine smell of him, intoxicating. A few minutes longer wouldn't hurt.

With Verrick held snugly in his arms, Lionel Parford was in no hurry to return to the house. She was letting him hold her and he hoped it was a sign she was beginning to trust him. She nestled so easily beneath his chin, he was loathe to release her.

"We must go back." Verrick's soft breath tickled against his neck.

He truly meant to release her and rejoin the family, but her inviting lips were so tempting, he lowered his head and covered them with his own. And to his delight, she kissed him back.

It was a Christmas gift more precious than any. With a sigh, she pulled back, shyly looking at her hands clutching the lapels of his jacket. She untangled her fingers and clasped them tightly in her lap. Lionel placed his large strong hand over hers.

"I'm not going to say I'm sorry."

Verrick peeped up at his solemn face.

"Shall we join the others now?"

She straightened her shoulders and nodded, standing and turning to avoid his gaze. She knew her feelings must be written on her face and didn't want to humiliate herself by revealing the love she was struggling to hide.

Silently they left the tropical warmth of the greenhouse and scurried through the cold drizzly rain to the house. Verrick hoped the streaky look to her cheeks would be attributed to the rain.

She managed to compose herself and smile, but Rachel wasn't fooled. She could read the signs. One would have to be blind to miss the lipstick on Lion's shirt collar and the tell-tale pink traces at the edge of his mouth. She exchanged a very pleased look with her twin brother. There was hope for Lion yet.

After a light supper, sleepy children were zipped into their winter parkas and one by one, the Parford children returned to their own homes.

Verrick thanked Lionel's mother and hugged her one last time.

"I'm happy you could spend Christmas with us, dear." Verrick basked in the kindness of the elderly couple.

Lionel was close behind her, helping her on with her coat, carrying her armful of gifts and storing them on the back seat of his car.

It was dark and raining but Verrick felt a peaceful contentment as the sleek car purred over the wet streets. This was a Christmas she would never forget.

They were both reluctant to break the spell of harmony between them. It was Christmas magic. Verrick wished with all her might it could last forever. But she couldn't keep pretending.

Lionel's voice entered her dreamy thoughts. "I know you have the final performance of the pantomime tomorrow, but on the next day, would you come to see that house you saw the blueprints for? I'd like to show it to you."

Had she imagined that invitation? No. It was real. He was looking at her, expecting an answer.

Verrick stammered, "I'd like that . . . but . . ." She hesitated before telling him about the Flying Doctors. Elly's sneering tones still rang in her ears. *Goody-two-shoes stuff if you ask me. No wages, no fun, not even decent meals or good hotels. Why do you do such things? You're an educated girl. You don't need to go traipsing off into the backwoods to earn a living. I can't understand what gets into you. It makes no sense.* But she also remembered Jenna's words, *Talk to the guy.* So she started again, "I'm going into a remote part of Northern British Columbia."

He wanted to see her reaction when she stepped into the house, hear her suggestions for paint colors, floor coverings, bathroom tiles, and all the little personal things that reflected the owner and made a home unique. He couldn't deny the fact—he was building this house with Verrick on his mind every step of the way.

"Will you be gone long?"

"Four days." He looked so disappointed.

Verrick was torn. She'd love to see that house in real life, not just as blueprints on paper. It was a dream home. She turned her head in the dim light inside the car. She opened her mouth to explain further but Lionel was looking at her with raised eyebrows and such a forbidding look, the words remained unspoken. It was a though she were a little girl again being scolded by her mother. A flood of black memories overwhelmed her. The fact that it was Christmas Day didn't help.

Lionel didn't pick up on her tortured expression. He was lost in his own thoughts. Visions of the driver of that Mercedes were flitting through his mind, alone with Verrick, for four whole days, in some romantic hideaway cabin. The way his dark eyebrows narrowed and he looked down his nose had Verrick shivering in spite of the car's heater. Rachel could have warned her about that look. It meant fireworks were about to erupt. Lionel was not pleased.

He was furious.

"I promised to . . ." Verrick stopped. He looked so fierce.

"I see." His voice was silky, quiet, but some deep emotion simmered near the surface. "Will you be alone?"

His tone accused her of some illicit rendezvous. No longer choked for words, Verrick erupted, "No, I'll not be alone!" She didn't know when to stop. Anger took over, all the bleak memories of Christmas past spurring her on. "I'll be with a man who doesn't raise accusing eyebrows and look down his nose at me."

Lionel Parford stared her down, then enraged her further by quietly repeating, "I see." He wanted to show Verrick the house he was building . . . what had he done to make her so upset? He cleared his throat to start again.

But Verrick, slumped down in her seat, was in no mood to listen. It hurt that Lionel could think she was sneaking off for some scandalous affair. Her voice was quiet, choked with threatening tears. "You don't see. . . . " She finished in a whisper, but he heard. "You may be perfect, but I'm not." She wasn't being fair. She knew that almost instantly. But some demon had taken over her tongue, lashing out as she'd never done in the past.

His voice was deceptively calm. He hated to see her tears and he couldn't bear to think of some other man touching her. He wanted to hold her in his arms and soothe away their misunderstanding. But he had to know. "Answer me this. Will you be spending the night with him?"

"Yes, I will," she sniffed. "And I don't plan to get much sleep." On previous trips with the Flying Doctors she'd worked long hours, well into the night, attending people who'd come long distances for urgent dental care. It was gratifying work. She said aloud the painful thoughts going through her head when she heard his sudden intake of breath. "You think the worst of me." She didn't know why that hurt so much but it did. The cheery Christmas lights of Westerly Place loomed ahead in the rainy night, less stormy outside than inside the sleek car.

Lionel Parford swerved into the underground parking lot, and before he'd pulled his key out of the ignition, Verrick had undone her seat belt and stepped out of his car. She was in tears, heading for the stairs, muttering to herself.

Lionel Parford caught a phrase as she stormed past him. "You could never love a dentist."

He bit down hard on his lower lip, glaring after her retreating form. Oh, but she was wrong! He wanted to race after her and shake her, make her see sense.

But he thought better of that idea. Verrick needed time to calm down. She was overwrought. This day filled with his boisterous relatives had been a lot for a quiet only child to handle. Things would look better in the morning.

He set her Christmas gifts outside her door and knocked softly.

There was no response.

Verrick had thrown herself across her bed and was sobbing her heart out, hugging the stuffed lion close against her chest. She loved him so much and he had such a low opinion of her.

The loveliest day had turned into a nightmare.

Chapter Ten

By seven o'clock on the morning of December twenty-
seventh, Verrick had carried her backpack and sleeping bag
into the lobby of Westerly Place. She was wearing several
layers of warm clothing and sturdy hiking boots. Her
satchel of dress-up clothes, with its wisps of colorful silks
and satins, was clasped in one hand as she heard the swish
of the elevator doors opening.

As Dr. Harris approached the lobby doors, he saw Verrick with a terrified look on her face. She had a death grip
on a bag she was holding up like a shield. But it looked
like no ordinary shield, a tantalizing hint of gauzy negligee
spilled over its top. A tall, angry man towered over her.
Thankfully, she saw Dr. Harris coming and opened the door
to let him in.

Lionel Parford looked this older, gray-haired man over,
scanning him from head to toe, dressed for the outdoors as
Verrick was, likely headed to some secret cabin in the
woods. It was not the driver of the Mercedes as he suspected and his words of apology had not been given. Verrick refused to answer her door or pick up her phone. Now
his furious eyes fixed on the man's left hand as he bent to
pick up Verrick's pack. A shining gold wedding band
glinted in the morning light. Fury overtook common sense.

He speared Verrick with his enraged gaze. His voice was chillingly sharp. "Is this the man you're sneaking off with?"

"Yes!" Verrick spat back at him. Her eyes were still puffy and her voice quavered.

"He's a married man. Does that mean nothing to you?"

"It means a lot." Verrick picked up her sleeping bag and stormed through the entrance doors to throw it in the back of Dr. Harris' car. She turned and cast one final glance at Lionel Parford standing in the doorway, feet apart, arms crossed across his chest, and a hostile look of sadness and pain scarring his handsome face.

Verrick lifted her chin, holding back tears, and stepped into the passenger seat of the waiting jeep. Immediately it pulled away from the curb, headed for the airport in the cold, damp, early morning fog that shrouded the streets and wrapped around Verrick's heart.

Bob Harris had the sense to remain silent. Verrick's puffy eyes and bleak expression said enough.

As they sped along the freeway, Verrick took several deep breaths, blew her nose, and composed herself. She had a job to do. The rest of the team counted on her.

Her companion could see she was hurting. He had a grown daughter of his own. His gentle voice expressed his concern. "Was that the boyfriend?"

"No, my neighbor."

"Nothing more?"

"Nothing!"

"Have you quarrelled?"

"He accused me of sneaking off with you for an illicit weekend."

Dr. Harris wanted to laugh, the very idea was ridiculous. He was a happily married man in his sixties. With difficulty, he kept a straight face. "Shows he cares, though, doesn't it?"

That stopped the flow of angry words building in Verrick's mind. She gave serious thought to her companion's comment.

The rest of the trip passed in comfortable silence, each gathering strength for the grueling task ahead.

The other two doctors were waiting on the tarmac as the pilot loaded their medical supplies into the small plane. Verrick had little time to think of anything else as they checked their provisions and went over their itinerary.

"I hope you're all rested. We're in for a grueling couple of days. Many of these people have never seen a dentist. Be prepared to work harder than you've ever worked in your life."

With that, they boarded the plane, strapped in, heading north over heavily forested islands dotting the strait, then higher over snow-covered mountains and frozen lakes with only occasional signs of habitation in the vast landscape.

The noise of the plane's engines made talking impossible, for which Verrick was glad. Dr. Harris had graciously pretended he'd forgotten the scene between herself and Lionel Parford. She wasn't up to explaining right now. She barely understood what came over her, slinging insults at him like she did. She only knew how much it hurt to have him think badly of her.

As the plane neared their first stop, a mining camp, Verrick fished in her bag for her tiara and gold satin cape. Dr. Peters, the young family physician along for the first time, stared, blinked to clear his vision, then stared again. Verrick tied her cape over her parka and produced her sparkling wand.

"The tooth fairy," she informed him in her sing-song voice.

His laughter bounced off the sides of the plane and the other two dentists joined in. Thus began a steady stream of patients with swollen cheeks, throbbing teeth, bleeding gums, and all manner of worrisome complaints. Seldom did they see a dentist and many conditions had been left too long without attention.

Verrick cajoled frightened children into the dentist chair

set up in a small room in the mining office. She reassured parents, filled teeth, and as the tooth fairy, instructed everyone on the importance of brushing and flossing. Each child left smiling, clutching a bright package containing a toothbrush, toothpaste and dental floss. The excitement of visiting the tooth fairy banished fears.

After briefly snatching a cup of tea and a sandwich for lunch, Verrick stayed on her feet until near midnight when her last patient roared off on his snowmobile after having a nasty abscessed tooth extracted.

She staggered into the meeting room that also served as a community hall. Several women of the village had prepared a potluck supper to welcome the doctors. The pilot, Matt Deacon, and her three colleagues had already eaten and were resting in camp chairs drinking beer with a group of men and women who didn't often get visitors from outside this time of year.

Verrick was hungry enough to eat anything—well not quite anything. She still remembered the frozen seal meat the Inuit children shared with her. She couldn't insult them by refusing their hospitality. But that oily, fishy taste remained with her to this day.

Much to her relief, she recognized a venison stew and dumplings and a glorious pot of tea. She ate, washed briefly in the company washroom, and was ready to collapse. But still, she sat up and made polite conversation with the few remaining residents who were eager to talk.

At long last, Bob Harris unfolded the camp cots provided for them. Their hosts got the hint and retired to their own homes. The pilot and doctors unrolled their sleeping bags and each selected a cot. Verrick didn't care that they were all grouped together against the wall. She had no thoughts of privacy. She was asleep the instant she took off her boots and lay down. It was Dr. Harris who zipped up her sleeping bag before he crawled into his own.

The same routine was repeated the next day, only this time in a church hall with trappers, loggers and their families as patients. That night they unfurled their sleeping bags onto the hard wooden pews and were exhausted enough to sleep, in spite of the frigid temperatures and howling wind swirling spirals of snow over the frozen ground that stretched for miles in every direction.

The next stop was a fishing outport where the galley of a fishing boat served as the dentist office. The patients were a hardy lot and Verrick felt gratified she could give the dental care they so desperately needed. She was getting tired and ready to go home, have a hot bath, and sleep in her own bed. Thoughts of Lionel crept in at the corners of her consciousness, but she threw herself into her work so vigorously, she was almost able to banish the pain of their angry parting.

The ship's radio crackled as Verrick was finishing a filling in the mouth of a seasoned old fisherman. His mate picked up the receiver.

"Samuels calling the Salty Sue. Over."

"Salty Sue here. Go ahead Samuels."

The fish boat captain looked puzzled. "That's the new fella over at the lighthouse," he explained, "hardly been there a year. Has a young wife with him. Must be pretty isolated in winter like this."

"Are the Flying Doctors in your area? I heard they were due this week."

"They're here all right. One fine dentist just filled the captain's tooth. And she didn't have to tie him in the chair. You got some emergency?"

"I don't know. My wife is pregnant, not due for another three weeks. She says she's fine but I'm not so sure. She looks pale and grimaces as though she's in pain but she says it's only the baby kicking. I'd be mighty grateful if one of those doctors could take a look at her."

Dr. Harris joined the group around the radio receiver. "That's three hours by boat from here," the captain explained. "You couldn't make it before nightfall." Bob Harris hated to admit to the hopeful man that three of the "doctors" were dentists. He motioned for Dr. Peters to take the call.

"Is your wife up to the trip here?"

"She doubles over if she walks more than a few feet. The sea's rough. It would be too hard on her."

Eric Peters confided to Bob Harris, "I say she shouldn't be moved. I'd like to have a few words with her."

"Samuels, can your wife come to the radio?"

There was a long pause, much static on the line, and what sounded like a deep sigh. "She doesn't know I'm making this call."

"There's a family physician here. He wants to talk to her. Tell her he's in the area making house calls. Get her to the radio."

While they waited for Mrs. Samuels to be fetched, Matt Deacon was called in to be consulted. "Can you get these doctors to the lighthouse? Sounds like Samuels' wife is in labor."

He looked out the porthole across the choppy gray sea. "The wind is up, rough seas, plenty of rocks near the light."

The fish boat captain pulled out his charts. "Look here, there's a sheltered cove east of the light, just around the point. Chances are, you could set your plane down there. It's a short hike up the cliff to the lighthouse."

Matt Deacon nodded.

The short wave radio crackled into life. "Samuels here."

"Here's Dr. Peters. He wants to talk to your wife."

"She's here."

"Mrs. Samuels, are you having pains at regular intervals?"

A faint voice answered, "Yes, doctor."

"How far apart are the pains?"

"Not regular . . . at first . . . but now about every ten minutes." Her voice trembled. She sounded very frightened and alone. Verrick's heart went out to the unknown woman in the distant lighthouse.

Dr. Peter's voice was very calm and reassuring. "That's

as it should be. Stay off your feet, take deep breaths, and I'll be there as quick as I can. You're doing fine, Mrs. Samuels."

The captain signed off and set down the headset. "Looks like you'll have to fly in, Matt. That lady doesn't have time to wait for you to get there by boat."

"I'll give it a try." He looked around at the four doctors gathered in the small ship's cabin. "Are you ready?"

All four answered at once. "Ready." They dashed off to pack their medical supplies and few personal belongings. Within twenty minutes, the plane was loaded and they were fastening seat belts for the short flight to the lighthouse.

Dark clouds hung low over the water. A frosty wind sent waves crashing against the rocky shore. Verrick shivered, frightened for the woman in need, glad that Eric Peters was here to help her, and oblivious to the dangers of landing a small float plane in blustery conditions near jagged rocks.

Matt Deacon said nothing, piloted the plane smoothly away from the fishing village and directly toward the lighthouse. The small cove was in the lee of the rocky bluff, the water fairly calm and no visible boulders or rock outcroppings. With his passengers holding their breath, fingers crossed and prepared for the worst, he set the plane down gently on the water's surface and glided toward the pebble beach where he cut the engine and spoke for the first time.

"We're here, folks."

They scrambled out of the plane, Eric Peters with his medical bag and the rest with camping supplies and foodstuffs. They didn't expect the lighthouse keeper and his wife to be in any condition to provide them with meals.

Matt secured his plane and led the somber party up the rugged trail leading to the light. It was steep and slippery with jagged rocks wet with salt spray. They were panting for breath when they reached the top where the barren, snow-covered rock leveled out. The light-keeper's house was visible toward the edge of the bluff.

Samuels was at the door to greet them, a bearded man

in his early forties, stoic by the look of him, not one to show his feelings. The speed with which he guided them to his wife's bedside, revealed his concern.

Dr. Peters went immediately to the woman's side, introduced himself and took charge with a confidence that was reassuring. Bob Harris, although a dentist, had attended the birth of his own three children. He assisted Eric Peters as he examined the patient.

Verrick had intended to find the kitchen and make them all a pot of tea, but the pleading look on the woman's face insisted she stay. Hers was the only female face Mrs. Samuels had seen in several months. The presence of another woman in the room seemed to comfort her and give her strength.

Verrick had never attended a delivery and didn't think she could be of much help. But Mrs. Samuels clung to her hand with a firm grip, she had no chance of slipping away. Eric Peters nodded his approval at Verrick as she spoke gently to the distressed woman, soothing chatter and calming encouragement. The woman could never have guessed that Verrick was as new to childbirth and as nervous as she was. It was a time her acting ability came in handy.

The labor pains came closer together and increased in intensity. Dr. Peters coached his patient through them, instructing her when to breathe and when to exhale. Verrick found herself breathing and exhaling in unison.

Dr. Harris was the one who found the kitchen and the pack of supplies Verrick had left near the door. Gratefully, Verrick accepted a mug of tea and some biscuits. Bob Harris patted her on the back. "Nice going, Dr. Grant." Then he winked. Knowing Verrick was a doctor gave Mrs. Samuels confidence. Neither she nor Bob Harris was going to tell the patient she was a dentist.

Later, Eric Peters described the birth as "straightforward, without complications" but Verrick considered it traumatic, exhausting and exhilarating. She felt she had worked as hard as the young mother now holding her infant son. Mr. Samuels downed the stiff glass of whisky Bob Harris put in his hand and was now able to enter the bedroom and admire his new son. Matt Deacon had kept the man distracted, asking questions, touring the lighthouse, and keeping up a steady stream of yarns and tall tales about his bush pilot days in the far north. Usually a solitary man, Mr. Samuels had never been more grateful for company.

Matt Deacon used the short wave radio to call his home office and inform them the Flying Doctors would be a day late getting back to Vancouver. They would leave the next morning. He'd radio in expected arrival time as soon as they were airborne.

As the doctors had been fed by appreciative local residents, they'd used none of their own food supplies. So, together, they prepared a feast to celebrate their successful trip and the birth of the Samuels' son.

Having eaten a satisfying meal, the weary group spread their sleeping bags on the kitchen floor of the lighthouse, in front of the wood stove, for what they thought was the last time before returning to the comfort of their own beds.

The trip home took longer than expected.

Chapter Eleven

"I'm sorry, sir. We're unable to make radio contact. Our lines are open to receive transmissions, but nothing has come through."

The furious scowl she received at this news made the airline receptionist offer further explanation. "There's a severe storm sweeping the whole B.C. coast with high winds, heavy snow and massive turbulence. It's not uncommon for transmissions to be blocked under such conditions."

The tall blond man continued his pacing across the bare floor, from one side of the terminal building to the other, with his hands clenched in tight fists as his sides, his eyes downcast, and his face strained. His whole body was tense, coiled, ready to spring.

But there was nothing he could do, no action he could take. The airline owner had explained the situation to him several times. It was impossible to send search and rescue planes out in weather like this. Visibility was next to zero and they had not as yet, pinpointed the area in which to search. But the man couldn't be pacified. He was in a raging temper, desperate to locate the missing plane and the five people on board.

"Did the plane send any distress signal before contact was lost? Was the pilot having mechanical problems?"

"No, sir. There was no distress signal, no hint of mechanical failure. As I've told you before, the pilot radioed in his flight plan and estimated time of arrival. At last contact he was nearing the northern tip of Vancouver Island."

"Damn! What fool kind of pilot is he?"

"Matt Deacon is one of our best, sir. He has fifteen years experience flying along the B.C. coast into mining sites, lumber camps, and every remote location you could imagine. He's never lost a plane or a passenger."

Lionel Parford snorted his contempt. "There's always a first time."

The receptionist's patience was wearing thin but she took pity on this distraught man. She watched him raking his fingers through his hair, grinding his teeth, wearing a track in the floor with his constant pacing. He looked at her with those bleak brown eyes. "Rest assured, sir. Matt will bring those four doctors home safely. He knows the coast like the back of his hand. They're probably holed up somewhere waiting out the storm. And if there's some medical problem, what could be better than having four doctors on board?"

This didn't have the desired effect. He didn't appear the least bit reassured. Nothing would calm this madman down until Matt Deacon and his four passengers walked through those doors into this reception room.

"If you give me your telephone number, sir, I'll call you the instant we have news."

He turned and glared at her as if she had lost her mind. "I'm not leaving." Her fearful expression made him add, "Can't you understand? She's out there somewhere in this terrible storm . . . cold, frightened . . . and I said the most terrible things to her. I can't go sit beside my cozy fire knowing what she's going through."

The woman behind the desk didn't say anything, but now she understood. One of the doctors was a woman, a very special woman the way this man was carrying on. She should have figured it out sooner, the moment he saw the report on the evening news and arrived here demanding to have everything possible done to rescue the plane.

There was not a sound, no movement, only heavy rain pounding the slick gray pavement of the parking lot where the abandoned cars of the missing doctors sat forlornly. She could do nothing to give him hope. She couldn't expect him to be rational—men in love never were.

It was going to be a long wait until Matt Deacon made radio contact, or the storm abated long enough to get rescue planes in the air. Until then, she was trapped in this terminal with a caged lion.

By the second day, even Verrick wouldn't have described Lionel Parford as Mr. Perfect. He had a two-day growth of beard, his eyes looked hollow, circled by bluish rings, his hair was tangled, and his clothes crumpled from sleeping in them in the terminal waiting room. He was a man obsessed. The staff, busy with their duties, avoided crossing his path.

Gavin had tracked him down and was with him now.

"Lion, you're not helping Verrick any by wearing yourself down like this. You aren't to blame. You can't control the weather . . ."

"I accused her of having an affair with a married man." The anguish in those bleary eyes was painful to look at. He didn't have to tell his brother how he felt about Verrick, or how much he regretted the angry words he'd hissed at her.

"She was going on a mission of mercy and I made it out to be some sordid encounter." He dropped his face into his hands and groaned. "Can she ever forgive me?"

Gavin patted his grieving brother on his back. "Come home, Lion. Have a shower and a hot meal. You'll feel a lot better." He wanted to give comfort but his brother was beyond reach. He mimicked Lionel's own strict tones. "Look at yourself. You'd scare the woman to death if she walked in and saw you looking like this."

Lionel grimaced, taking in his grubby appearance and cold surroundings. He opened his mouth to speak but suddenly stiffened, alert to the slightest sound.

A barely perceptible crackling, no louder than the scratchings of a mouse, had Lionel up out of his chair, and in a few long strides, leaning over the panel of instruments behind the controller's desk.

Gavin looked at his watch—five a.m. Through the glass doors he could see stars still twinkling in the night sky. Stars? That meant the cloud cover had lifted, the day would dawn bright. Lion's ordeal should soon be over.

That scratchy sound was the most beautiful thing Lionel Parford had ever heard. It broke the hushed silence. "Deacon here. Do you read me?"

The three people in the room beamed. The tension in their weary bodies eased as they strained to hear the fuzzy transmission.

"We read you loud and clear, Deacon. What is your location?"

"By my reckoning, we're in a cove south of Port Alice. The wind is down, the sea is calm. At first light, we're coming home."

"Do you require assistance?"

"None whatsoever. Thought I'd radio early in case you were sending out Search and Rescue. It'd be a wasted expense."

"Rescue you, Deacon? It never occurred to us! No trap's been set to catch an old bear like you."

Lionel Parford choked back his outrage. Of course they were sending out Search and Rescue. Verrick's life was at stake. How could the radio operator tease at a time like this?

Gavin thumped Lionel on his back. "See, what did I tell you? Everything's fine."

Hearing Gavin's voice, the radio operator remembered the other people in the waiting room. "Are your passengers all safe?"

"Snug as a bug in a rug. They've had an unexpected camping trip, but no harm done."

"There's a fellow here who'd like to talk to Dr. Grant."

"What? Now? It's five o'clock in the morning! Decent people are still asleep."

"He says it's urgent."

"It'll have to wait. When it's daylight, we've loaded the plane and are set to leave, I'll radio back. Over and out."

The ever-increasing drone of a small aircraft approaching from the north had Lionel Parford transfixed on the small dock, his hand shielding his eyes, as he scanned the gray sky for the first sight of the long-awaited float plane. He was undaunted by the crisp cold of a winter morning or the bone-chilling dampness that kept the flight crew waiting for the overdue plane huddled for warmth inside the terminal building.

A brief flash of light reflected off metal rewarded Lionel Parford's lonely vigil. The engine sound was louder now as Matt Deacon circled to make a landing on the calm muddy water.

Verrick felt the quivery stomach sensation of the plane losing altitude. She peeked across Dr. Harris' chest to take in the welcome sight of smooth water and a solid dock. Camping out on a deserted shore in a snowstorm had drawn the five occupants of the plane close together. The sight of the dock was the first confirmation that their ordeal was at an end.

Her breath caught in her throat as she recognized the tall figure with his chin lifted, eyes skyward, as he watched the descending plane. He was as tense with anticipation and unexpelled breath as Verrick herself.

Bob Harris noticed the direction of her gaze, and the wide-eyed look of shock on Verrick's face. He patted her hand and spoke in his best, soothing, bedside voice, "That must be your neighbor."

Not trusting her voice to speak, Verrick nodded, never

taking her eyes off the figure on the dock. She didn't know what to expect when she tumbled off this plane in clothes she'd worn continuously for three days, knotted hair, filthy black fingernails, muddy patches on her knees, and over all, smelling of wood smoke, perspiration, and kerosene.

She didn't know what to expect, but she drank in the sight of Lionel Parford, fresh from the shower, cleanly-shaved, blond hair immaculately combed, overcoat pristine, jeans washed and free of stains, even his shoes were polished. She watched his lean length pacing the planks of the dock like an angry father whose daughter hadn't been brought home on time for her curfew.

Verrick exhaled and slumped against Bob Harris. He patted her hand reassuringly. "We're home safely, Dr. Grant. He's bound to be a bit worked up after we were lost without a trace like that. Give him time to cool down. Everything will work out just fine. Trust me."

Verrick's dark-rimmed eyes stared up at him doubtfully. He took both her hands in his as the floats touched down on the surface of the water and the plane turned to taxi into the dock. For a young woman who had been so brave and resourceful these past few days, Verrick Grant was nervous. It had nothing to do with the plane landing.

"It's going to be all right, Verrick. You'll see."

At the moment, all she could see were those chocolate brown eyes boring into her. She trembled, squashed between Bob Harris and Eric Peters. Without their support, she would have cowered beneath the seat.

Bob Harris had no further chance to comfort Verrick. The small plane had touched the edge of the dock. The door was yanked open, two powerful arms reached in, unbuckled Verrick's seat belt, grabbed her by the shoulders, and drew her out across the plane's float onto the dock, before anyone could utter a word or even catch their breath.

While Matt Deacon did a final check of his instrument panel, then assisted the three male doctors out of the plane, Verrick melted into Lionel's outstretched arms. His lips covered hers in a kiss that was neither brotherly nor that of a neighbor. It was downright sensuous, searing the helpless girl with his brand, so possessive no one dared interrupt.

But Verrick wasn't fighting. Her arms were around his neck, clinging to him and returning one kiss after another as though no one else was standing on the narrow dock, wanting to unload the plane and move on up to the terminal out of the drenching rain and cold morning air.

Three airline staff in overalls and warm parkas hurried down the ramp to help unload luggage and medical equipment from the plane's hold. The back slapping and cheerful greetings went unheeded by the two people locked in each other's embrace.

Once started, Lionel Parford couldn't stop kissing the woman who'd wrenched his heart out and taken it down with that plane. He ran the back of his hand along her jaw and stroked the faint trails washed by tears on her sooty face. She smelled like a smoky campfire. It smelled wonderful.

He meant to assist the men he was vaguely aware of, unloading the plane beside them. But her warm responsive lips drew him back to caress them. He couldn't get his fill.

Matt Deacon made a noisy display of clearing his throat. The plane was unloaded. Everyone was shuffling up to the terminal. Icy rain was coming down in bucket loads. It was time to make a statement to the press.

He hated to drag Verrick away. Although, he could think of it as saving her life for a second time. If she didn't drown in the rain soaking her to the skin, she'd likely suffocate, unable to draw breath with that man's lips covering hers. Matt coughed loud enough to get attention.

That press statement had to be made. The airline's reputation required a confirmation—neither pilot nor plane was at fault for the delayed arrival. The safety record of the company would be enhanced by the pilot's actions to ensure the well-being of his passengers.

None of this mattered to Lionel Parford. Verrick was here in his arms, safe. He was vaguely aware of Matt Deacon making a commotion on the dock, coughing and sputtering, trying to get their attention. Slowly he lifted his head, still holding Verrick securely in his arms, then turned to glare at the unkempt pilot in a battered ski jacket, a full growth of beard, and dirty clothes that had seen better days.

Matt grinned his lopsided smirk. "A reporter and TV crew are waiting for us to give a statement. Dr. Grant will have to be present to confirm that no harm came to her." He shifted his weight restlessly, anxious to be done with all this fuss and get back into the air. He was at home flying across vast wilderness into isolated communities, not facing microphones and cameras and giving press releases. His job demanded it; but he didn't have to like it.

Verrick's glazed look focussed on Matt, edgy and ill-at-ease now that they were back in civilization. They owed their lives to his wise actions. She smiled at him with that warm beguiling enchantment that could get the most terrified patient to open his mouth for her.

She eased back from Lionel's side. "We're coming, Matt. Let's get this over with." He nodded his agreement and turned to saunter up to the terminal building and the group of people gathered inside, out of the downpour.

Verrick grasped Lionel's hand and followed the gruff man whose kind heart was no secret to her. The reality was seeping into her befuddled senses. They were home. Lion was here beside her. She hadn't apologized, she hadn't said a word to him. Too much was happening at once. But something must be said.

She glanced up at the rain-slicked face so dear to her and whispered a short phrase that expressed all that was in her heart. "I love you."

Her feet were in motion, Lion's steady arm supporting her around the waist. To Matt Deacon, Lionel Parford looked more in need of support than Dr. Grant. He looked like he'd gone fifteen rounds with the champ. "Punch drunk" the guys in camp called it. Dr. Grant's young man couldn't take his eyes off her. He'd have tripped and fallen into the water if she weren't holding his hand tightly. The seasoned outdoorsman shrugged and pulled open the door to the terminal.

Light bulbs flashed, everyone asked questions at once, and a statement was made to the reporters. The five weary travellers smiled politely for the cameras, answered questions, then called a quick halt to the interrogation, claiming an anxious need to get home to their families, have a long hot shower, and enjoy a decent meal.

Lionel Parford watched as the five bedraggled companions hugged each other and filed out into the rain-soaked parking lot, quickly retrieved their personal belongings, unlocked their waiting cars, said their final farewells and drove off on this miserable wet day. Even though gray clouds blanketed the sky, dense and dark, threatening more rain, Lionel Parford's heart was filled with sunshine.

Bob Harris hugged Verrick as she picked out her backpack. He had driven her to the airport but doubted he would be driving her home. "See. What did I tell you? Everything will work out just fine." He looked over her shoulder at Lionel Parford watching them from a discreet distance. He wasn't a man who'd take kindly to other men hugging his Verrick. Dr. Harris kissed Verrick on her cheek, then opened his car door. "Your Lion is ready to pounce. Don't keep him waiting."

Verrick was left standing with her heavy backpack at her feet, in the middle of an abandoned parking lot with incessant sheets of cold rain washing over her. Lion was at her side. "My car is over here." His arm at her back guided her to the other side of the building, her pack slung over his shoulder.

White flecks of snow were added to the rain now. Verrick turned her face up into the cold downpour, letting it wash away the smoky soot and grime of the past few days. She licked her lips, the salty taste of perspiration mixing with the icy rainwater.

That flick of her tongue over those delectable lips was all it took to destroy Lionel Parford's careful plans. The bouquets of lilacs at his apartment, the champagne chilling on ice and the dinner he had planned for her, were forgotten. He intended to give her time, let her recover from her ordeal. She needed a chance to reconsider those words whispered in the heat of the moment.

But those intentions vanished when he saw the tip of her tongue sweeping across those lips, a temptation that freezing rain and a cold empty parking lot couldn't dampen.

He dropped the clumsy backpack to the ground and took her in his arms. "Verrick, darling. When that plane went down, my heart went with it. I knew then how much I love you." His deep voice quavered with emotion. "I don't want to face another day without you in it."

There, shivering in the pouring rain, on the slick wet pavement, he took her hand in his, bent on one knee, and sent waves of heat over her with his passionate dark eyes. "Will you marry me?"

Scruffy in the clothes she'd lived in for the past several days, choked by the tight lump in her throat and blinded by the tears filling her eyes, Verrick gazed at the man on bended knee before her. She was oblivious to the bleak surroundings or the frigid rain plastering her hair to her face and soaking into her jacket in widening damp plops. Her bleary eyes looked at Lion, his hand warm and strong holding hers. It was all too much.

She shook her head and snuffled.

Seagulls screeched as they circled overhead. The splatterings of slushy rain against the pavement sounded loud to his ears. It could have been the sound of his heart being torn apart, so devastated was the look on Lionel Parford's face.

"I do love you," Verrick sobbed. "But I can't marry you."

Now it was Lionel's turn to shake his head, rain dripping from his soaked hair, ice melting from his frozen hopes. She did love him.

His voice was soft and coaxing. "Why can't you marry me?"

Verrick was shaking. Her blue eyes were swimming. She sounded so miserable. "I'd make your life unbearable." He shook his head once more. "Yes, I would. You're so perfect and . . . and I'm not."

That was enough. He wouldn't listen to another word. He stretched up to his full height, threw his overcoat around her and placed a finger over her lips to silence her.

As the raindrops darkened his pale blue shirt to a deeper shade, he held her against his chest and pushed back the dripping hair from her face. "No, my love. I'm not perfect."

He gently kissed her wet lips. "It will take me a lifetime to learn to be the husband you deserve."

That brought her tears into full flood, soaking the front of his shirt that wasn't already drenched by rain.

He lifted her chin and kissed the tip of her nose. "Will you give me a chance?"

Shivering, her head firmly held in his grasp, Verrick couldn't deny herself the dream she'd longed for.

"I love you Verrick. Will you marry me?"

"Yes," she whispered, unable to say another word.

They sealed that promise with a kiss, standing in a rainstorm in the middle of a parking lot on a cold winter day.

To them, it felt like blazing sunshine on a tropical isle.

Epilogue

The first rays of morning light poked in around the edges of the floral curtains, brightening the rose-colored master bedroom and announcing the beginning of another glorious sunny day. Birds nesting in the giant maple tree sat in a row on the upper branches preening themselves, soaking up the heat of the sun's rays, chirping with good cheer, joining the chorus of robins in full voice in the apple trees. The fragrance of lilacs, lovingly planted in profusion, filled the room with the sweet smell of summer.

Verrick snuggled deeper beneath the down comforter, blissfully warm, safe and protected, surfacing into wakefulness as she burrowed her face closer into the bare shoulder supporting her. She sighed. This surely must be heaven.

"Good morning, Mrs. Parford."

The deep voice reverberated through her, making her wriggle with pleasure at the familiar sound. Her hand resting on his solid chest stroked the soft mat of hair, but she was too comfortable to open her eyes.

"I know you're awake. Your breathing has changed and your heart is beating faster." He kissed her forehead where it rested so close to his chin. "What could you be thinking about?"

Verrick pressed closer into his warm side and lifted her
mouth to kiss his whiskery chin. "I love you, Lion."

She could feel the jiggling in his chest. He was chuckling.

"You're not going to tell me, are you?"

"I will," she murmured, planting a trail of kisses down
his neck.

"Now would be a good time." She knew he was smiling
at her, holding back outright laughter. His voice was gentle
and coaxing, very happy, as though he already knew.

"I tried last night but you were so . . . so amorous."

He bit his cheeks to keep from laughing. "I wasn't the
one who. . . ."

Verrick pressed her hand across his lips. "Well . . . I saw
Dr. Peters yesterday."

"Yes, I know. You told me that part."

"Well . . . he examined me."

"And . . . ?"

"And he took a scan."

He turned on his side to look down into her early morning blue eyes. Getting information out of her was worse
than pulling teeth. Didn't she realize by now that he loved
her, no matter what she had to tell him? "What did the scan
show?"

"There are two heartbeats . . . and two bodies."

He wrapped his arms around her and kissed her thoroughly. "That's wonderful!"

She'd known he'd be pleased. Holding back her own
delighted smile, she lowered her eyelashes and grumbled,
"Easy for you to say. You're not the one who's going to
gain thirty pounds and be kept awake at night by *your* twins
wrestling inside me."

She tried to sound gruff, but her smile gave her away.

"*My* twins?"

"You're the one to blame. It's not inherited from me,
there are no twins in my family."

He threw his head back and laughed, hugging her closely against his bare chest.

The bedroom door opened a crack, and hearing the deep-voiced laughter, two little boys ran into the bedroom—two identical little boys in striped flannel pajamas, with blond hair and brown eyes, the image of their father.

"Mommy, Daddy," the two-year-old voices squealed as they leapt onto the big bed and cuddled in beside their parents.

Lionel Parford grinned at his wife and teased, "No twins in your family, darling?"

She joined his laughter, secure in his love.

There were now going to be two sets of twins in their family.

Life with Mr. Perfect was more wonderful than anything she could have imagined.

MARLBOROUGH PUBLIC LIBRARY

3 0453 0000 9741 3

Marlborough Public Library
35 West Main Street
Marlborough, MA 01752
Phone (508) 624-6900 Fax (508) 485-1494
www.marlborough.com/library/index.html